FIRE!

Melanie finds her own imaginary world
a far more comfortable place than the
real world around her. A mystery
surrounds the disappearance of her
father. Why will no one talk about him?
Why is it she can't remember? Melanie's
quest for truth leads her into danger.

VERONICA HELEY is the author of more
than 20 books for children and adults.

FIRE!

Veronica Heley

A LION PAPERBACK
Oxford · Batavia · Sydney

Copyright © 1990 Veronica Heley

Published by
Lion Publishing plc
Sandy Lane West, Oxford, England
ISBN 0 7459 1851 4
Lion Publishing Corporation
1705 Hubbard Avenue, Batavia, Illinois, 60510 USA
ISBN 0 7459 1851 4
Albatross Books Pty Ltd
PO Box 320, Sutherland, NSW 2232, Australia
ISBN 0 7324 0166 6

British Library Cataloguing in Publication Data
Heley, Veronica
  Fire!
  I. Title
  823'.914 [J]

  ISBN 0 7459 1851 4

Library of Congress Cataloging in Publication Data
(Applied for)

Printed and bound in Great Britain by
Cox and Wyman Ltd, Reading

CONTENTS

1

CONGRATULATIONS
ARE IN ORDER

Da-da! Da-da!

The fire engine made Melanie jump. It alarmed her
so much that it sent her into one of her dizzy spells.
She leaned against the shop window as the engine
swept around the corner and disappeared.

She had been walking home after drama club with
two of her school-friends. Not that Melanie was an
actress. She'd have died if they'd made her get up
on stage and act. But she was fascinated by the lights
and the make-believe of it all. She'd hung around so
much after school on Thursdays that they'd grabbed
her for prompt duties. It was the highlight of her
week.

Melanie liked being quiet in a corner, but helping
to make things happen. And she would dearly have
loved to be accepted on equal terms with those who
made things happen on stage.

She knew they merely tolerated her, because she
was useful and a good listener, but that was all right
by Melanie. They let her walk home with them,
almost as if she belonged. Only they couldn't under-

stand why she was so frightened of fire engines.

Neither could Melanie, as a matter of fact.

Now Jo said, "Are you all right?" She said it in the way you asked a little sister or brother if they were all right when they fell down and scratched themselves. Half concerned, and half cross because they'd been an idiot.

"Yes," said Melanie, trying not to wheeze. She didn't feel all right, but she knew they thought she was daft about fire engines.

Jo looked at Shiroma, and shrugged. Jo said, "Race you to the lamp-post!"

They raced off, laughing, bumping their school cases and their swimming things in plastic bags along beside them.

Melanie didn't mind being left behind. On these occasions, she actually preferred it. She told herself to breathe deeply. In and out. In. And out. The dizzy feeling went away, but her legs were still weak. Had the fire engine gone down her road? Would she turn the corner and find it outside their house, with ladders out and hoses playing on the front, and flames tearing holes into the roof?

And people screaming.

She often had nightmares about fire, and always there was someone screaming. Trapped. There was nothing as frightening as fire.

She turned the corner, but wouldn't look ahead. The others would have disappeared by now, anyway. Jo lived down the next road along, and Shiroma in the same road as Melanie, but much further on.

Melanie said to herself, *If I can step on five paving stones without treading on a crack, there won't be a fire engine in the road.* She managed it, and looked up. There was no fire engine.

A few steps more and she brushed through the overgrown hedge on to the path which led up to their front door. The gate had been propped open long ago with a stone, waiting for someone to get around to mending it. Only there wasn't anyone around who was good with a hammer and nails, and there never seemed to be enough money to get someone in to mend things. Her mother could hardly mend a tear in a school blouse, never mind a broken gate.

"Oh, throw it away," her mother would cry. "I'll get another on Saturday, or whenever I can manage to get to the shops. Life's too short."

Aunt Bet would take the blouse and mend it, and there would be a lot of sighing and cursing under her breath while she did so. Aunt Bet was used to picking up the pieces, but she made sure you knew that she didn't enjoy doing it. Particularly now.

Aunt Bet drove up in her battered Renault 5, parked untidily, and started hauling the week's shopping out of the back. Aunt Bet worked flexitime in an old-established grocers in the town, so she could almost always be home when Melanie got back from school.

Lots of people thought Aunt Bet was Melanie's mother because they both had longish, straight fair hair and light eyebrows, and because Melanie's real mother, Karen, was so young-looking and full of energy. The only things Melanie and her mother had in common were bright blue, china blue eyes.

"Did you see a fire engine?" asked Melanie, helping to get the food into the kitchen.

"No," said Aunt Bet. "Now don't start that nonsense again. It's not funny any more."

Aunt Bet was cross again. She'd been cross a lot, lately. It was something to do with the shop and her job, but if Melanie asked she got her head bitten off — so she didn't ask.

The bag containing fruit split, and apples and oranges rolled over the floor.

"Oh, I could spit!" said Aunt Bet, making no move to pick them up. She was crying.

Melanie picked them up, silently, and went out into the back garden to feed the birds. She loved the birds, and she loved the back garden.

The front garden was small, with room for only two aged rose bushes, speckled with black spot, and an overgrown privet hedge. The back garden was something else. There were lilac and forsythia bushes around the sagging fence, lots of roses, and a tiny sump of a pond where there was frog-spawn, and where Melanie had once seen a dragonfly. Or perhaps she had dreamed it.

But she hadn't dreamed the roses. There were masses of roses, and she knew the names of some of them, even. The back garden was Melanie's responsibility, and she spent a lot of time there, worrying about whether she ought to prune things back and, if so, how. She worried that the roses would die on her if she didn't treat them properly, but this year they seemed better than ever, producing daily showers of colour.

Melanie couldn't bear to let all that beauty die and be lost for ever, so Aunt Bet had suggested that they could make some pot-pourri with the petals. Every day Melanie went round collecting the petals, and put them to dry in a paper bag on top of the boiler.

She was happy in the garden. She spread out crumbs on the bird-table which she had improvised high up in a big rose bush. The sparrows were already flying around, waiting for her. They knew she fed them every day, and they watched for her coming. The cats couldn't climb the rose bushes to get at the birds. It was all very satisfactory.

"Melanie! Come on! I want to get supper out of the way, so's I can get to rehearsal! And you haven't started your homework yet!"

Melanie jumped. She hated being shouted at. It made her mouth turn dry and sour, and set her shivering. But she knew she'd been quite a time in the garden, so she went indoors and tried to eat the food her aunt slapped on to the table.

"You know I need to get out early today," grumbled Aunt Bet. "You know the drama club is the only thing that keeps me going . . . "

Melanie knew. She understood completely why Aunt Bet set so much store on the town's drama club. Didn't she have much the same feelings herself, even if she was only "prompt" in the school productions, while Aunt Bet got small parts and actually went on stage?

Suddenly Aunt Bet pushed her plate aside, and covered her eyes, delving for the roll of kitchen towels. Melanie put down her knife and fork but didn't ask what was the matter, because she knew. The shop was not doing well. They'd put in a new manager, and he was going to reorganize, but everyone knew the writing was on the wall, especially since a new supermarket was opening up just outside town.

There were going to be redundancies. Aunt Bet was afraid.

" . . . and there's a note for you, in the letter your mother sent me."

Aunt Bet was resolutely dishing out ice-cream for them both. She spooned it into her mouth, with one eye on the clock.

11

"She's enjoying this film; they're in first-class accommodation this time, and it's not too hot. Glorious weather, of course. What I'd give to . . . well, never mind. We can't all be clever, can we? But she won't be home till the end of the week, she says. The film's running late."

The film always did run late, in Melanie's experience. Her mother was an assistant director in an independent film unit. She could be in Sri Lanka one minute, and Southend the next. She was more likely to be in Sri Lanka than Southend. She wasn't home, much.

"She says in her letter," said Aunt Bet, throwing dishes into the sink, "that David's going to meet her at the airport and bring her home. That's the third time in a row. I wonder . . . Well, you can't blame her, can you? You like David don't you, Melanie?"

Melanie pushed her sausage around her plate. She wasn't hungry. She didn't reply to Aunt Bet's question. David was all right, she supposed. Her mother seemed to like him. He had a big car and smiled a lot. Sometimes he gave Melanie a ride in his car.

"I've got to go," said Aunt Bet, in a hurry as usual. "Don't let anyone in, pet. Sorry I've got to leave you with the washing-up, but . . . Don't watch TV too late, and remember, I've switched the hot water on for a bath for you."

Melanie said "OK," and waited until Aunt Bet was gone and the house was quiet again.

Melanie could breathe more easily when she was alone in the house. She turned off the radio which Aunt Bet always had blaring away, and let the quietness drift back around her. From the house on the right she could hear the faint sound of a game show on the TV. On the left she could hear the old woman

12

next door coughing. She thought she could smell something burning, but it was only a piece of fat on the gas stove.

In a minute, when she was quite sure she wasn't going to be disturbed, the cat might come out to play.

She picked up her mother's note and took it through into the front room. She didn't open her mother's letters any more because she knew what would be in them. Her mother had a portable word processor which she took everywhere with her. It was useful for work, of course. It was also useful for letter-writing. Her mother would write one long letter to Aunt Bet, and then she'd cut out all the interesting bits of gossip and send a shortened version to Melanie. As a matter of duty, really. All the news was in Aunt Bet's letter, and Aunt Bet always passed that on.

Melanie hated having these cast-off letters. That's how she thought of them. Cast-offs. They were "Oh dear, I haven't written to the child, and I suppose I'd better," sort of letters.

That sort of letter didn't deserve any attention at all on the part of the person who got it. Melanie lifted the lid of the oak chest in the window of the front room, and slid the note inside. There were a lot of other notes in there from her mother, all unopened. No one ever opened that chest, except to put in things they didn't need but which were too good to throw away.

She went upstairs, into the tiny room overlooking the front garden that had been hers ever since they'd moved into this house two years ago. Melanie couldn't remember where they'd lived before, but knew it was on the other side of town somewhere. She'd been ill that year, and her memory of that

13

time was hazy. The old school, the old house, old friends . . .

Well, they said, she was lucky to be alive. She wondered if she was, sometimes. Life was so . . . unfinished.

But she liked her present room. There wasn't room to swing a cat there — only her cat wasn't a live one, but a big black china cat with a clover leaf on its back, which lived on the window sill.

"Pussy cat, pussy cat, where have you been?" said Melanie.

The cat gave her its mysterious, wouldn't-you-like-to-know smile.

"Have you been up to London to see the Queen?" said Melanie.

The cat grinned, and flexed its claws.

"Have we had a good day?" asked Melanie. "What did we see today, then?"

The cat's eyes narrowed to green slits. "We saw something beginning with F."

"Flowers?"

"Stupid!"

"Fairies!"

"Idiot!"

"Fire engine!" guessed Melanie, and sat on the bed, feeling weak.

She could hear the fire engine coming down the street, with its bell clanging. Then she realized that it was the telephone, ringing in the hall below. She tried to hurry down the stairs, but her legs wouldn't go as fast as she wanted, and she banged herself against the wall before she got the phone off the hook.

"Is that you, Bet?" Her mother's voice floated across the miles, bringing Melanie back into sharp focus. "Oh, blast, I forgot, it's her night out, isn't it?

Melanie, is that you? You sound snuffly. Have you got another of your colds? Well, never mind that. I wanted to tell Bet, but you can be the first to hear. Congratulations are in order. Tell her that, will you? And, of course, you're both to be bridesmaids."

Melanie felt her breathing accelerate.

"Are you there, Melanie?"

"Yes," said Melanie, sitting on the stairs. "But I don't understand . . . "

"What a silly girl you are. I'm sure I've given you enough hints. I'm going to get married again, of course. What else?"

Married? Melanie couldn't take it in. She heard the distant call of the fire engine, and the clang of its bell as it passed along the street, and that blotted out what her mother was saying.

Melanie put the phone down.

And then there was nothing.

2

BLACK CAT, WHITE CAT

"Melanie! Melanie, whatever is the matter with you!"

Aunt Bet's face was close to hers, but her voice seemed to be coming from a long way off. Then the voice closed up with the face. Melanie tried to sit up, but couldn't.

And then she could. She had pins and needles. She was sitting on the stairs, propped up against the wall, in a very awkward position.

"You frightened me! What on earth . . . and the dishes not done! And look at the time! It's a good thing I came back early. Karen said she'd ring. I forgot, and then they didn't need me, so I . . . "

Melanie nearly said, "Who's Karen?" But realized just in time that Karen was her mother. Melanie thought there was something she ought to tell Aunt Bet about her mother.

" . . . so I think you'd better see the doctor. We've been putting it off long enough . . . " said Aunt Bet.

Aunt Bet was scolding Melanie, but that was all right. Melanie knew that Aunt Bet loved her after her own fashion. Not as a mother loves her daughter, no.

But in an exasperated, Karen's-always-doing-this-to-me, I-like-the-child, but-why-do-I-put-up-with-it sort of way. Aunt Bet was always saying, "If I had my time again . . . "

Aunt Bet had wanted to go to live in London when she left school, but first there was the orphaned younger sister Karen to bring up. So Aunt Bet had stayed. It was Karen who had gone out into the world eventually, leaving Melanie to be looked after by Bet.

Sometimes Karen had said to Bet, "Well, you could have gone, if you'd really wanted to."

And Bet would say, "And what would have become of you and Melanie if I had?"

It gave a rough underlay to her care for them.

"You don't eat enough to keep a flea alive," said Aunt Bet, helping Melanie into bed. "First thing, I'll ring work and get time off, and take you to the doctor's. Right?"

Melanie lay on her back and looked up at the ceiling. She knew what the doctor would say, because he'd said it before. She could see the cat silhouetted against the street lights outside. The curtains in Melanie's room were unlined, but it didn't bother the cat whether it were night or day.

"You're in dead trouble," observed the cat, furling its tail more tightly about itself. "You're going to have to be more careful in future. You might even have to eat more of their horrible food."

"Bless and save us!" observed another, comical-sounding voice. The white cat appeared on the window-ledge beside the black one. The black one hissed and moved along so that they weren't in contact with one another.

"What a fuss about nothing. Glory be!" said the white cat.

Melanie snuggled down into her pillow. She knew the white cat wasn't really there. She knew it was really in her head, and not on the window-ledge. But she liked the white cat. She liked its way of sending up even the most tragic situations.

"Can't you be serious for once?" snarled the black cat.

"Can't you see the poor thing is worn out?" said the white cat. "Let's sing her to sleep. Hushabye, baby . . . "

The white cat stretched out his forepaw, and gently touched the girl on her forehead . . . or that's what it felt like to Melanie.

Her eyes closed, fluttered open, and closed again. She slept.

Aunt Bet marched Melanie into the doctor's surgery as if to a court martial. Left, right, turn, sit in the chair. Keep your mouth shut, and let me do the talking.

The doctor was a rounded little man with gingerish hair, what there was of it. He was rather nice. His eyes flicked up to Aunt Bet, as she stood like a guardsman on parade behind Melanie, and then down to Melanie, as she sat wishing herself elsewhere.

" . . . and I came back to find her in a dead faint. And she's hardly eating anything . . . You know what she is!"

The doctor did indeed know what Melanie was like. Her file lay on the desk before him. A thick file for a child of her age. He sighed, stroking his cheek, measuring her listlessness, the dun colour of her skin, the thinness of her hands.

He said, "Well, shall we examine you, Melanie?" He did all the usual things, pounding this and punching that, and making her breathe in and out. Then he washed his hands, and said to Aunt Bet, "Perhaps you would wait outside?"

Aunt Bet pinched in her lips, but left Melanie alone with the doctor.

Melanie felt her eyes fill with tears. The doctor handed her a tissue, and patted her hand. Then he put his arm around her shoulders and gave her a quick hug. He wouldn't have done that with Aunt Bet there, thought Melanie. But it did help a bit.

He said, "My dear, this has got to stop. I've known you since you were a baby. If we don't tackle this situation now, you're going to end up with more than just asthma."

"You make it sound as if I could help having asthma."

"Mm. It's all linked, or so the specialists believe. What I say is that if you don't eat enough to keep a sparrow alive, then we have to do something about it."

"I don't feel hungry."

"Hm. How are you getting on at your new school?"

"It's all right."

"Friends?"

"Some."

"Close friends?"

"Not really."

"Sport?"

She didn't answer that one.

He started to write on her card, and she looked out of the window. It looked like rain. Autumn was a windy time of year, whirling the leaves off the trees, whirling them all into winter. Melanie hated winter.

He said, tearing off a prescription, "You'd better take these three times a day; see if they'll help. I'll want a word with your mother when she returns, if you're not eating properly by then. When is she due back?"

"Tomorrow night maybe. Maybe the next day."

It was raining quite hard by the time they got to school.

Usually when Karen was expected back, Aunt Bet came home from work early to polish everything in sight and jam flowers into a vase. But this time when Melanie arrived back, Aunt Bet was standing at the front window, gazing outside like a sleep-walker. The room hadn't been dusted, nor the carpet hoovered.

Melanie went out into the garden to feed the birds. There was a greyness in the air, and the birds had already gone to sleep. Soon the nights would draw in, and though the roses might continue to bloom for a while, their colour would fade. She would come home from school in the dark and would no longer be able to spend time in the garden.

Melanie stood there, looking up at the sky, feeling empty. She was waiting, just as Aunt Bet was waiting. The white cat came slithering through the long grass, and purred around her legs. Melanie smiled.

She heard Aunt Bet's voice raised in welcome, and went back into the house. Her mother gave her a smothering hug and passed on into the living-room, shedding duty-free bags, a leather coat, handbag, airline holdall and a rather pervasive scent. Her mother's voice was high and sweet, her diction perfect. She never raised her voice, yet could be heard all over the house.

She wore a lot of glass bracelets which she had acquired on a trip to India, so that she tinkled and twinkled as she moved. She was rarely still, and hardly ever stopped talking.

" . . . so the plane was early, and was I glad to be out of that. Oh, my dear, what pretty flowers, I think they'd go beautifully in that . . . shall I? No, of course I'm not too tired, but I must admit a cup of coffee, not that awful instant muck, but the real . . . Oh, thank you, darling! How would I manage without . . . and darling David, do give my lovely sister a kiss . . . "

A shriek, and she clutched at Melanie's shoulder. "My dear, how peaky you look! Give her a kiss, too, David!"

David, who was a big man with awkward-looking bones clothed in an expensive suit, put his arm around Melanie, and pulled her towards him. He was smiling, but Melanie thought he was as embarrassed as she was by all this Togetherness.

She let him kiss her, but didn't kiss him back, and felt she could breathe more easily when he'd let her go.

Aunt Bet said, arranging flowers, "I had to take her to the doctor in the week. He said she's getting anaemic, got to eat more. As if I haven't tried. And if she doesn't pick up soon, we've got to think about taking the matter further . . . specialists and things. And he said that with her asthma, we've got to watch she doesn't get over-tired."

"Oh dear," said Karen, in her high, polite voice. She looked really worried for a moment, as if she didn't know what to do with her hands. Then she remembered that she'd been going to get a cigarette out, and started diving in her pockets for her lighter, while making what she felt were the right responses. "Oh dear! What a bore for you both. Melanie, darling! You really must try to eat more, and not to be a bother to your aunt. Come here, dear, and let me have a look at you. Where did I leave my cigarettes?"

Melanie shifted backwards out of reach, but there was David standing in the doorway, grinning at nothing in particular.

Karen picked up her coat, patted the pockets, and delved into her airline bag, talking all the time. " . . . and where did I put my . . . oh, darling, did you bring my bag in from the car? So sorry, but I think I put the presents in . . . "

She broke off to seize Melanie by her shoulders, and give her a hug. "Isn't it all wonderful? Aren't you excited? You remember David's house, don't you? Oh no, perhaps you didn't come with me when . . . but you'll see, it's just perfect, and you can have your own room decorated just as you please. I did wonder, at first, with his own children being away at university, whether he'd want to lumber himself with another, but I said I was sure you wouldn't be any trouble, so . . . What's the matter with you, Bet?"

Bet had not gone out to make the coffee as Karen had intended. Bet had sat down on the settee, her knees and ankles together, looking angry.

Bet said, "They're closing down the shop, making it self-service. They have to give me a month's pay for every year I've worked there, but at the end of the month . . . after all these years!"

"Oh!" Karen suddenly looked her age. She sat down beside Bet and put her arm about her, but it didn't look as if she were trying to comfort Bet. More as if she felt she ought to, but wasn't sure how. Bet stared straight ahead.

Melanie could hear David heaving Karen's suitcase into the house. Melanie went into the kitchen and put the kettle on for her mother's cup of coffee. Not instant coffee. Ground coffee. She got out the little round lacquered tray which her mother had brought back from the Far East. Everything had to be just so for her mother. If Melanie were to spill a drop of milk, there'd be ructions. She began to have difficulty with her breathing. She fought to breathe easily, but couldn't. The room blacked out. She slid to the floor and let everything ease away.

Aunt Bet drove them all out to David's house the next afternoon. The sun was shining, but the sky was heavy with menacing clouds, racing before the wind. It wasn't any too warm.

They passed out of the grimy end of town and into the clean countryside. There was a feeling that mist was about to form in the hollows of the landscape, but the trees had not started to shed their leaves yet, and it was what Karen insisted on calling A Perfect Autumn Day. There was a semi-circular driveway into David's property, which contained a large house in best black-and-white, mock-Tudor, stockbroker style.

"Lovely, isn't it?" said Karen, getting out of the car and shaking her dark hair loose in the sunlight. "The swimming-pool's at the back; heated, of course. There's room for four cars in the garage. There is a staff flat over the garage for the housekeeper. She seems very nice. And he gets a woman to come in to clean, and help with dinner parties and so on."

She strode ahead of them into the house, giving a peal on the doorbell as she went. Melanie and Aunt Bet looked around with mistrustful eyes, and then followed her.

A wide, long-windowed sitting-room overlooking

23

a huge stretch of lawn ("he has a man to take care of the grounds, of course!"), a morning-room, a study, a dining-room.

Melanie lost count of the rooms.

They went up a wide staircase, the sort you see people in evening dress gliding down in old films. The master bedroom, as big as a ballroom. The guest suite.

" . . . and this is your room, Melanie."

It was a very large room, with windows overlooking the pool and the sweep of countryside beyond. A room with white-painted, gilded furniture in it. A bathroom led off it. The curtains were floor to ceiling, lined and interlined. There were pink ostrich feathers in a pink vase to match the pink curtains, carpet and bed-linen.

It looked like something out of *House and Garden*. It didn't look like a teenager's room at all. Melanie tried to imagine the black cat sitting on the window-ledge, but couldn't.

Karen and David drifted out along the landing. Aunt Bet said, "Well!" and sat down on the bed. Her hand caressed the pink silk scatter cushions that lay on the bed.

Melanie felt all adrift.

"Aunt Bet, are you coming to live here, too?"

"No," said Aunt Bet, with a mixture of elation and anger. "I'm going to strike out for myself at last. We'll sell the house and split the proceeds and with my share, I'm going south. I've always wanted to. They say there's plenty of jobs down in London."

"Couldn't I come with you?"

Aunt Bet looked away, awkwardly silent.

Melanie sat beside her aunt, and touched her skirt.

"Couldn't I? I can't stay here. I couldn't stand it. It would make me ill."

Aunt Bet moved along the bed to avoid Melanie's hand. "It's out of the question. If I had you with me, I couldn't get on, make a living. Besides, it's my turn to get away. You'll be all right, you'll see. It just takes a bit of getting used to, all this."

Melanie said, under her breath, "I hate him! I hate her! I won't come to live here! I won't, I won't!"

3

HOUSE FOR SALE

"Where are you going for half-term?"

Jo and Shiroma were talking about the forthcoming holiday, and Melanie was listening in, as usual. Shiroma and her family were going to France, if their father could get away from work. Jo said they were going to stay with cousins, where they could go horse-riding.

Melanie couldn't keep her end up in this conversation. She thought it must be wonderful to be Jo or Shiroma. They weren't afraid of anything, not even of fire engines. And they attracted friends like flies.

Take Claire, for instance. Claire was new to the school, having recently moved into the road in which Jo lived. Claire's mother was pretty well off, and Claire didn't think much of their comprehensive school. Claire thought her mother would probably send her to a posh private school next year.

Normally in a comprehensive school, this sort of talk wouldn't get much of an audience, but there was something about Claire which made them want to admire her, even when they disapproved of what she was saying.

Because Claire was good at everything. She was good at lessons and good at sports. She was brilliant in the drama club, and had walked straight into a big role in the new production. It was a role which Jo had thought was going to be hers, and it was a measure of Claire's personality that Jo had actually been heard to agree that it did suit Claire better.

They were doing *The King and I* for their Christmas show that year. Jo could sing and dance quite well, but not as well as Claire, so Jo was going to be the juvenile lead, and Claire would be Anna. They had asked Melanie if she would like to be one of the ladies or even one of the children because she was so small. But Melanie had felt ill at the thought of going on stage, and clung to her prompt book.

That was all right by the others. They couldn't quite understand how Melanie could be so, well, droopy. But they realized she had asthma, and they tolerated her. She was, after all, useful to have around. To fetch and carry, and listen.

"Hi! Wait for me!"

It was Claire, running along behind them. They had just reached the turn into Melanie's road, and they stopped to let Claire catch up with them.

Melanie wondered whether to make an excuse and leave them. Jo and Shiroma wouldn't want her hanging around when they had Claire to talk to. She looked down her road, and nearly fainted.

A sign had been nailed to the gate-post of their house, saying *FOR SALE, View by Appointment Only*.

Melanie dropped her school bag, and Claire ran into it.

"Ouch!" said Claire, rubbing her ankle. "What did you do that for, clumsy?"

"Sorry," said Melanie. Or rather, she tried to say it, but couldn't get the word out. She could see Claire's angry face, and the faces of the other girls turned towards her, looking annoyed. Did they think she'd done it on purpose? Claire was saying something else to her, but still Melanie couldn't speak.

It was all that Melanie could do to remain standing upright. Claire pulled a face at Melanie, stretching her mouth wide and wiggling her fingers above her ears, tongue lolling. Jo and Shiroma laughed. Claire laughed.

Melanie's eyes were open, and with one part of her mind she understood that Claire had got the sympathy of the other girls . . . but it was impossible for her to react.

She closed her eyes for a moment. When she opened them again, the three girls had gone. Melanie felt incredibly tired, and a bit weepy. She plodded along until she discovered she hadn't got her school bag. She went back for it. Every step was an effort.

She passed under the sign without glancing at it, and went indoors. Her mother was there, smoking, and chattering away on the phone. The living-room was littered with half-drunk mugs of coffee, expensive magazines, scripts, books, pencilled notes on the backs of envelopes, the word processor. Clothes. A cashmere sweater had been flung at a chair and missed it to slide on to the carpet. Melanie picked up the sweater and stroked it. How beautifully soft it was, as soft as the fur on her little white cat.

"And what's wrong with you, misery-guts?" said her mother, putting the phone down on one call, and immediately dialling another number. "Blast. Engaged."

She slammed the phone down, stubbed out one cigarette, and lit another.

"Well, come and talk to me. I haven't had a good talk with you in ages. I miss you, you know, when I'm away. I think of all the things you must be doing, and . . . why don't you ever write and tell me what you're up to, eh? Other girls do. Your aunt tells me you're in the drama club. What are they doing?"

"The King and I."

"Oh. That's nice. Have you got a good part in it?" She picked the phone up, and tried her number again. "Still engaged. Can't think why they don't get some more lines put in. So, how was school today? I suppose I'd better get round to see your Head sometime. David said he'd stump up the fees for a boarding school for you next term. God knows, you need a bit of help, judging by your last reports. I hope you've been working hard to . . . Blast, still engaged."

She put the phone down and looked vaguely around for an ashtray. Melanie picked one up from the muddle on the floor, and held it out for her mother to use.

"I did think, once," said Karen, looking at Melanie as if she really saw her, and really wanted to communicate with her, "that you took after me, and would be able to fight your way to the top, as I have. But your school reports, darling, aren't . . . are they?"

"No," said Melanie, knowing they certainly weren't.

"It's hard to know what to do for the best. You do understand that, don't you?"

"Yes," Melanie realized that Karen was concerned for her, in her own way.

"I mean, why do you get such bad reports, darling?

The teachers say you don't seem to care, that you're totally uninterested . . . "

"I know," said Melanie, wincing.

"But why, darling? I mean, it's supposed to be a good school — of its type."

"I get so tired," she said, knowing it was an inadequate explanation, but not having any other to offer.

"Then you should take the pills the doctor gave you. Bother!"

The phone shrilled under Karen's fingers, and she picked it up, her voice and manner changing back to what it usually was. "Oh, darling! I've been waiting for you to phone back about the . . . yes, the budget is a shock, I know, but . . . "

Melanie tidied up the room, while her mother went from one "quick" phone call to another which was desperately urgent, darling! It warmed Melanie to know that her mother did care about her, even if business had to come first.

Later, when Melanie was washing up in the kitchen, her mother came in and actually picked up a tea-towel to dry a mug.

"Sorry we were interrupted, darling, but needs must . . . Now what was I saying about your schooling? Well, I'm not going to say a word against Bet. She's been very good to you. I must ring round, contact some people I know down in London. I ought to be able to wangle her an interview or two, at the very least. Get her a better job than . . . what are you crying for?"

"I . . . I don't want the house to be sold. I don't really have to go and live with David, do I?"

Karen laughed, a sweet, meaningless sound. "What else, love? Do you think you could live here all by yourself, pay the mortgage, look after yourself, or something? Bet's going to need half of what the house sells for, to set up for herself. And God knows, I could do with the money to buy a car and a few good clothes . . . I haven't a thing worth looking at and . . . Come on, love, it's not the end of the world. Anyone would think this place was a palace. It isn't even as if we've lived here very long, only what, two years, isn't it? I've never liked it, but Bet had to do it all — selling our old house and her flat, and finding somewhere quickly . . . with me still out in Australia. You won't remember much about it — you were in hospital — but I can tell you, it was the worst time of my life."

"But I like it here! I don't want to move!"

"Oh darling, don't be silly! You can't like it that much! It really is a dump!"

Melanie could tell her mother was trying to be kind and loving, but to her sharp ears there came another message: "Don't press your luck, girl!"

"Think of the lovely times you'll have when we're married," said Karen, brightly, setting the one mug that she'd dried on the edge of the table where anyone passing by would knock it off. She waved the tea-towel around above her head, "Olé! How about Spain for our Christmas holidays? David's been so generous, even more than I'd expected. His first wife died of cancer. So sad. We'd known them for ever. I liked her. And his kids, well, I don't suppose you remember them, but they used to play with you when you were little, before they went away to university and that. They're happy about their father marrying again. I suppose it may have been a shock to you, although, God knows, I did try to break it to you gently. You must have guessed . . . "

"No, I didn't," said Melanie, rescuing the mug and hanging it on the hook under the cupboard.

"Well, darling," said her mother, trying to be gentle, but with the note of irritation coming over strongly, "you must realize that I have my own life to lead. I've always been fond of David, of course. And then he was so marvellous to me after . . . Honestly, even then my friends said they wondered if he wasn't more interested than . . . well, of course he wasn't, then. But one thing does lead to another, and it's a long time now since . . . and then, there's all the other side of things that you'll understand better when you grow up."

She put an arm around Melanie, her bracelets digging into her daughter's ribs. "My word, but you are thin! All skin and bones, still. At your age I was getting quite a figure. Not too much, of course. One doesn't want too much at your age, or it all turns to fat later. I suppose you take after Bet. She was a late developer. When we buy your bridesmaid's dress, perhaps we'd better ask them to put a bit of padding up top, eh?"

"I don't want to be a bridesmaid."

"You'll do as you're told, child." Now the pretty voice had a shrill note in it. Melanie felt cold. And very much alone.

Melanie lay on her bed and scribbled in her rough book. She had finished her homework more or less, and if she liked she could go downstairs and watch TV. Aunt Bet was out at her drama club. Her mother had gone out in the big car with David.

"Pussy cat, pussy cat, where have you been?
Bet's going to London to visit the Queen.
Pussy cat, pussy cat, why can't I go, too?

I'll miss her. No one else cares. I can't leave here. I can't. I can't . . . "

She felt the usual choking feeling begin to rise inside her, and fought it down. She'd been having more and more of these spells lately, and the doctor had prescribed an inhaler for her asthma. It did seem to help. She got it out now, and puffed away.

The black cat flexed its front paws. "We *are* down, aren't we? Are we down enough to do something about it, or are we going to sit around moaning and let them get away with it? Are we mouse, or man?"

"Mouse," said Melanie. "Definitely, mouse."

"In that case," said the cat, "I'll turn my back on you." And he did.

"Sorry, cat. Please, come back and talk to me."

The black cat twitched its tail, but didn't reply.

The white cat slid slowly into view. He put out his front paw, and dabbed at Melanie's cheek. "Bless us and save us, it *is* down, isn't it? Cheer up, lovey. You think you're all alone in the world, that no one cares. But that's not true. Remember what I told you . . . "

"Remember, remember the fifth of November," said the black cat, suddenly taking an interest. "Gunpowder, treason and plot."

"I hate fireworks," said Melanie, shivering.

"Of course you do. Every sensible cat hates fireworks. When there's fireworks around, their providers make sure they're not left out in the cold winter night. The cats are looked after, taken indoors, cuddled and given special treats to eat."

"I'm not quite sure I follow you," said Melanie.

"Don't listen to him," said the white cat, becoming agitated.

"Think about things burning," said the black cat, lashing its tail at the white cat. "Think about charred wood. Think about the glow of the fire, the blackness. Remember how it smells?"

"Don't listen!" cried the white cat, but he was fast disappearing and Melanie ignored him.

"I'm beginning to get the idea," she said to the black cat.

"You *are* slow," said the black cat, but he looked pleased, nevertheless.

Melanie leaned back on the bed. "If I'm ill, they won't bother me about moving or anything. Things will stay the way they are. And I can make myself ill by thinking about fire."

She smiled. The black cat smiled.

But the white cat had disappeared.

4

PAPER DOLL

I am a shadow, thought Melanie. *I love Aunt Bet, I really do. When I think of her, I feel all hot and angry because she doesn't love me as much as I love her. I wish, oh, I wish . . . But she won't take me with her. I wish she would. I could put up with everything else, if only she would.*

The hall was full of tea-chests and boxes. Aunt Bet was packing to remove her things to London. Karen had found her someone to stay with, one of her friends in the television industry who was glad to have a lodger for a while. Aunt Bet's things were all going into store, until she could find her own, unfurnished accommodation.

There were squabbles now and then between Bet and Karen, as to whether the best tea service was Bet's or Karen's. Likewise the cooking things, and the towels.

Melanie hated to hear them argue. It made her feel sick.

She told Jo all about it one day, when Shiroma was off sick with a cold, and Claire was kept back for extra hockey practice.

"I try not to mind, honest; I do try," said Melanie, finding Jo an unexpectedly sympathetic listener now that she was on her own.

Jo made faces at herself in a shop window as they passed. She said, "Look, this is nonsense. You've got to talk to your mum about it; make her understand. I mean, I can see why you don't want to have things broken up around you. At least, I can see it in a way. But surely, you'll be a lot better off in future. This David sounds all right, and for the first time ever your mum won't have to worry about making a living and can spend time with you."

"I can't see it happening," said Melanie. "I'm trying to be fair, but I know she thinks I'm an awful nuisance. I mean, it's her that talks about sending me away to boarding school, not David."

"Boarding school might be all right."

"For some, yes. Not for me. I need to be quiet, I suppose."

"Mm, privacy and all that. I see what you mean. You're not the type, are you?"

They got to the corner of Melanie's road, and halted. Jo was fingering the cross that hung on a thin chain round her neck.

She said, "Look, it's none of my business, but if I were in your shoes, and if I'd got into a bit of a state about something, and the parents couldn't help for some reason . . . well, I'd know what to do about it."

"What?"

"Well . . . " Jo swung her school bag to and fro. "What I mean is, he's always there, always the same. 'He doesn't alter, when he alteration finds . . . ' Don't you like that poem? The one that says true love doesn't alter when he finds his love has changed?"

36

"Shakespeare," guessed Melanie. "But I haven't a lover . . . "

"Oh, not that sort of lover. Don't you know who I mean?"

Melanie couldn't think why Jo was going red. She seemed really embarrassed, which surprised Melanie, who hadn't thought anything could embarrass Jo.

"Jesus. You know!" said Jo, almost shouting. Then she realized she'd been shouting, and glanced around to see if anyone had noticed.

Melanie began to get angry. "Oh, come on! Nobody believes in . . . "

"I do!" said Jo. "If you did, too, then you wouldn't be in such a state. He's always there, and he loves you, and is just waiting for you to turn to him for help. Haven't your parents ever taken you to church? Haven't they ever told you stories about him?"

Melanie was going to say "No!" very loudly, when like a faint scratchy echo in her ear, she heard someone talking about Jesus.

"Dunno," she said. "Maybe. Yonks ago, when I was little. But we've never been to church while we've lived here."

"Well, that's not so long, is it? I remember you moving in, just before we all started at this school. Two years ago, it must be. Didn't you go to church when you were at your first school?"

"Can't remember," said Melanie. "You know, I was sick for a long time, just before we came here. I don't remember much about what happened before."

"Rheumatic fever, or something? Glandular fever? I had a cousin once, who had to drop out of school for a whole year, and she was always tired, like you. I do think you ought to go back to the doctor's, you know.

Make him do some tests, find out what's wrong with you. I mean, you're drooping all over the place, aren't you?"

Melanie was silent. Aunt Bet was always saying the same thing, but she was leaving it to Karen to do something about it, and Karen was always too busy.

Melanie lifted her hand and said, "Well, see you! And thanks for listening."

Jo hesitated, and then came running after her. "Look, don't get me wrong. I believe in Jesus, but I've not been going to church long, and I don't know all the answers. Only, I could do a bit of praying for you, if you like."

Melanie stared at Jo. It was nice of Jo to think of praying for her, but if you didn't believe in it, then what was the point? Only Jo had been so kind, and Melanie didn't like to reject her offer out of hand.

"Oh, be like that, then!" said Jo, swinging away. "See if I care!" And she ran across the road and disappeared.

Melanie paused in the doorway of the sitting-room. Her mother looked up, smiled and continued with her phone conversation. There was a script on her lap, and the remains of one spread about her on the floor. Karen gestured to Melanie that she would like a cup of coffee. Melanie went round the room, collecting all the used mugs and cups and saucers she could find, and retreated to the kitchen to wash up and make the coffee.

When she got back, her mother was just off the phone, making notes with furious energy on her script. She said, "Sit down, darling; I want to talk to you . . . let's hope the phone doesn't ring again for a moment or two . . . Wait! I'll take it off the hook. That's better. Now . . . "

She leaned back, and looked at Melanie. She was smiling, but her eyes were unfocussed. Evidently she wasn't wearing her contact lenses that day. She got out her glasses, the ones she hated to use, and put them on. Now her eyes were sharply in focus, very business-like.

She patted the settee beside her, and Melanie sat down, moving a pile of magazines and papers on to the floor.

Karen put her hand on Melanie's knee, and left it there. "We don't know one another very well, do we? Well, all that's going to change. I've been so accustomed to flying here and there, always being at the beck and call of the telephone . . . it'll seem strange to be in one place most of the time. David didn't want me to go abroad again, so I've been trying to get a job at the local TV station. That's why I've been so busy, trying to clear up my old job, and getting my thoughts together for a new one."

"Do you have to work, still?"

"I'd go mad, otherwise. I've always worked. Always been busy. Always earned my own living. You won't understand, perhaps, but if a woman doesn't make the most of herself in that way, well, if the marriage goes wrong, or something happens, then she's stuck. I know. So you see, you and I have both got a lot of adjustments to make."

"Yes," said Melanie, seeing that it was true.

"Now I'm worried about you. We all are. David and I are going to be out at work all day, and we don't want you to be alone too much, so we think it best that you go to boarding school."

"No!" said Melanie.

"It's funny, but David said the same. He said some kids liked it and some didn't, and he didn't think you would. I really don't know what to do for the best. Perhaps the doctor could advise . . . "

"I don't want to go for any more tests."

"No." Karen frowned, and then smoothed the frown out with the pencil she happened to be holding. "Not tests, exactly. I've been talking to the doctor, and he says you're not picking up as you should. He thinks it's time to talk to a specialist."

"What sort of specialist?"

"Well . . . you know . . . a specialist in what makes people tick, what makes them ill."

"You mean a shrink?"

"A psychiatrist, yes."

"No!" The very thought made Melanie feel ill.

"No, I agree," said Karen. "I don't think it's at all necessary. I think that we're all going through a bad patch, what with Bet leaving, and the wedding coming up, and selling the house and all. I think that once we're settled, you'll feel better. And I don't want you to be sent to the psychiatrist. It goes down on your school records, you know, and then when it comes to applying for universities . . . "

"Me? Universities?"

"Yes, of course. You're not stupid, and when you're over this patch, I'm sure you'll be up there with the best. So that's OK then, is it? Oh, Lord, look at the time! I promised I'd ring . . . but I've got to collect the wedding invitations from the printer, and then . . . Get your coat on, darling. I'll call a taxi and . . . hurry up!"

"Where are we going?"

"I've got a fitting for my wedding dress in half an hour's time, and you can have one at the same time

40

for your bridesmaid's dress. The same as Bet's, only in a different size, of course . . . "

Melanie looked at herself in the dress, and drew back. It was a scaled-down version of the one Bet would have, in pink, with blue ribbons. It had a full skirt over a crinoline petticoat.

"My, my. And how old are you?" said the fitter, expertly pinching back the silk to make the bodice fit.

Melanie didn't reply. She knew how the rest of the conversation would go. My, my! Aren't you thin? My, my! You should eat more, dear. My, my! And what school do you go to? There, there! Doesn't she look lovely!

Only she didn't look lovely. Looking at herself in the mirror, she saw that the dress almost stood up by itself, and that it didn't belong to her. She thought it was like a paper dress that you put on a paper doll, fitting the paper tabs over the paper shoulders . . . and then you took it off and tried on another.

Only Melanie wasn't being given any choice in the matter.

"How about this? Is it a trifle long?"

Her mother swept out of her cubicle, trailing lacy flounces and yards of white ribbon. Melanie was sure her mother thought of herself as "a vision".

Karen pulled her long, dark hair up and back. "Shall I wear my hair up or not? I can't decide. Melanie, what do you think? Yes, dear, you look very nice . . . but don't you think, a little pad-ding . . . where it counts? Yes, I think I shall wear my hair up . . . "

Melanie wanted to scream. THIS WAS ALL

41

WRONG. This couldn't be happening. She closed her eyes and concentrated on burning. On flames, and fire. And smoke.

She began to choke.

That was the first time she deliberately made herself ill.

"Now," said the new English teacher, "what's so funny about the name Georgina? I will not have you teasing new girls — or boys — for that matter. Georgina as a name derives from George. You, Joanne. Can you tell me what man's name was altered to give you yours?"

"Um, John, I suppose, Miss."

"Right. A great many of our Christian names are derived from the names of great Christians of the past, both male and female. Claire, you are one. Anna, of course. Luke, Matthew, James and so on. Put up your hands if you were given the name of either your father or your mother. Melanie, you are not attending! Melanie! That's better. What was your father's name?"

Melanie gaped. Her mind was a white blank.

Claire, sitting directly behind Melanie, giggled. "She doesn't know what her father's name is!" Claire's voice carried. Everyone heard.

A lot of the class giggled, but the teacher looked worried. "Come on, Melanie. You must know your father's name!"

"I bet she hasn't got a father!" said Claire, *sotto voce*.

Melanie stood up, short of breath. "Please, could I go outside for a moment?"

The teacher sent her out. Melanie leaned against the wall outside, trying to breathe normally, puffing away at her inhaler. Normally the inhaler helped. Today it didn't.

The bell went for the end of the lesson, and Melanie was surrounded by curious faces. "She doesn't know who her father is!"

"Leave her alone!" That was Jo. "Can't you see she's not well?"

"She makes herself ill. There's nothing wrong with her, really, except she's illegitimate. She's what they call a bastard!"

"I'm not!" cried Melanie, fighting for breath.

"Bastard, bastard!"

"Stop it!" cried Melanie, thrusting at Claire's shoulders.

Claire grabbed the inhaler from Melanie's out-thrust hand and ran off with it, whooping, down the corridor.

Melanie felt herself begin to strangle, and slid to the floor with a bump.

Jo and Shiroma ran after Claire, shouting to her to come back.

Suddenly there was a nasty, thick silence. The sort of silence which announces a teacher has come upon the scene of a crime.

Melanie lifted her head slowly, panting. The teacher was taking the inhaler from Claire and telling her to report to the Deputy Head. The inhaler was put into Melanie's hand and she was helped to the First Aid room where she sat down and tried to control her breathing.

But it was no use. Even the inhaler didn't help, today. At lunchtime the school secretary rang for Melanie's mother to fetch her daughter home.

Karen was not pleased. David had bought her a new car, which she drove, accelerator and brake, all the way back home. She said she'd had to interrupt an important meeting to fetch Melanie, and another buyer wanted to come round the house, which was looking like a Tip, and the garden was a Jungle, and Now This!

Melanie staggered from the car to the kitchen and sat there, with her hands over her ears.

"Listen to me!" Karen snatched Melanie's hands from her head. "I won't have this nonsense, do you hear? Either you go to the doctor or . . . no, you don't want that, do you? No, of course you don't. So pull yourself together, girl. You're just making yourself ill, you know that, don't you? Just because I've got a chance of happiness at last . . . Well, let me tell you, madam, it won't work. Either you change your ways and drop this act of yours, or . . . I can tell you, this sort of behaviour is not helping you with David, and it's he who has the final say about your going to boarding school, so it's up to you now, isn't it?"

Melanie realized her mother had a point, but she couldn't seem to help herself. She had to know.

"I can't seem to remember. I did have a father, didn't I? I'm not a bastard. I'm not! What was his name? Tell me about him."

"What?" Her mother changed tack, forgetful even of the cigarette she was lighting. "No, of course you're not a bastard. Whoever . . . ? You don't want to think about him, darling. You know it only makes you ill."

She fidgeted about the kitchen, picking up clean things and putting them away, stashing dirty mugs in the sink.

"That's the point," said Melanie. "It's not knowing that's so awful. When I try to think . . . "

"Now, we don't want to start that again," said

44

Karen, emptying the drainer into the garbage. Before Melanie could stop her, Karen had inspected the bag of dried rose petals, and dumped that in the garbage, too.

"Oh!" cried Melanie, jumping to her feet. "Don't!"

"Don't do what?" said her mother, thrusting the petals down among the yukky mess, and snapping down the lid.

"That was my rose petals . . . "

"I can't have rubbish hanging around . . . look at the place!"

"But I was collecting them for . . . "

"If you were collecting them for the wedding, I'm sorry, but I prefer nice, hygienic paper ones. And anyway, I don't think there were nearly enough. Oh, I'm sorry if you'd set your heart on it, but really, you could have warned me! I didn't know they were important, did I?"

Melanie ran, wheezing, up the stairs, and collapsed on her bed. Her mother followed her, still complaining.

" . . . and that's another thing, I asked you to tidy up this room and look at it!"

She picked up a sweater which had fallen on the floor, and threw it into the open wardrobe. The flying sleeve of the sweater caught the tip of the black cat's tail, and it tipped slowly, head first, over the edge.

Even then everything might have been all right, but Karen, not noticing the cat, and moving rapidly about the room putting things to rights, trod backwards on to the frail china shell with her high heel.

Melanie tried to scream a warning, but too late.

"Blast!" said Karen, annoyed at the damage. The phone rang and she ran down to answer it.

Melanie lunged towards the cat with outstretched hands. It lay in a dozen pieces, smashed. Voiceless.

Melanie lay on the floor, her eyes wide open, seeing nothing.

She didn't hear her mother call up that the buyer had postponed his visit and that she was going out. She didn't hear the front door bang, or the car start up.

She lay there, silent, voiceless, with her eyes open.

5

WHO DID THAT?

Next day she got up, washed, dressed, did her hair and went to school. At least, part of her did.

Later, much later, the doctors told her that when the cat was broken, she had gone into shock. They used a lot of medical terms which she didn't understand, but what it boiled down to was that her mind had gone into second gear.

Her eyes recorded what was going on around her, but it was no longer real. It was like watching a film. An almost silent film. She could hear the shouts of children in the playground, but they were muffled.

On either side of her walked the black cat and the white. Sometimes one of them would run ahead, and wait for her to catch up. They talked to her a lot. Melanie listened to them. They were more real than the real world.

One part of her mind was still connected to the real world, and that part of her mind got her to school, listened to the lessons, and wrote down the questions for homework. But the other part of her mind had an even busier time, because it was trying to solve a mystery. The mystery of what had happened to her father.

She thought, although she could not be sure, that she remembered what he looked like: big and fair. And sounded like: deep and mellow. But the more she tried to remember, the more her memory refused to obey her.

In the break she drifted over to Jo and Shiroma. They were talking about the previous evening's rehearsal. Melanie had missed the rehearsal, and the producer had been furious. He'd said that Melanie was always letting them down, and if she didn't have a really good excuse he'd have to get someone to take her place.

Shiroma looked at Melanie, expecting her to be upset, but Melanie couldn't be upset about something which was no longer of any importance to her.

Jo said, "Leave her alone, Shiroma, will you? You can see she's not well."

"I'm all right," said Melanie, and smiled at them both. She really did like them, especially Jo. She'd love to tell them all about what was happening to her, about the cats, and her father . . . But she realized they wouldn't understand. So she smiled at them.

Claire came up, bouncing a rubber ball. Claire had pretty well got the ball to do as she wanted. Melanie smiled at Claire, too.

Claire didn't smile back, but moved between Melanie and Jo, edging Melanie out.

Melanie didn't mind. Then she remembered that Claire's parents were divorced. Her father had gone off with some woman or other to live in Spain. Claire was very open about it. Claire said she had never really liked holidays in Spain.

Jo's face came close to hers. "Melanie, are you all right?"

"Yes, I think so. Jo, do you know what happened to my father?"

Someone said, "She's blooming flipped!"

Jo's face faded away.

Melanie thought, *I suppose my father must have divorced my mother, and gone away, perhaps to Spain. I wish he'd taken me, too.*

She went to the far end of the playground, to be by herself. Suddenly there was a rush of feet and something whizzed to the tarmac behind her. She turned to see what it was, but she was too slow, too uncertain on her feet.

Crack!

Melanie screamed and screamed, a high thin sound. Then she felt strange and fell down, flop. The black cat and the white cat crept into her arms and went to sleep.

"Wake up, wake up, Melanie! That's it . . . you're quite safe!"

"Did she faint, Miss?"

"What happened, Miss?"

"She was startled by the firework. And I'd like to know who it was who threw it. There, now. Drink this water. Find her inhaler will you, one of you? Now stand back. Give her air. Did anyone see who threw the firework?"

"No, Miss. Not me, Miss."

The teacher helped Melanie to her feet with un-friendly efficiency. Melanie got the message: she was being a nuisance, causing an upset in the dinner hour. Melanie felt confused. The cats were talking in her head, and they were talking so loudly that she had difficulty in hearing what people in that other world, the playground world, were saying.

"Melanie, are you all right, now?" That was the teacher.

Melanie turned her eyes on the teacher, and tried to concentrate. Something was being asked. Ah, she had it. The teacher wanted to know if Melanie had seen who had thrown the firework. The firework was there, burned out, lying on the tarmac. But Melanie hadn't seen anyone. Or had she? Out of the corner of her eye? She had heard a rush of feet, and had half-turned, slowly . . .

The black cat said, positively, "It was Claire, of course."

"Now, now. You don't *know* that," said the white cat, anxiously.

"It was, it was, it was! I know it was!"

"But you didn't actually see! If you say it was Claire, then it might get her into trouble, and you know you shouldn't tell lies about people."

Melanie said, "It was Claire. I think."

The teacher snapped to attention. "Ah. Right. I'll deal with Mistress Claire. Now one of you, take Melanie to the First Aid room . . . and Shiroma, get the office to telephone Melanie's mother to fetch her home. There's the bell. Come on, all of you. The bell's gone."

Shiroma helped Melanie to walk back into the school, but her back was stiff, and her arm unhelpful. She said, "You know, Melanie, I don't think it was Claire, because I saw her over the far side, playing with some of the boys, just before the firework went off."

"It was her. She hates me. She's always trying to get me into trouble."

50

Shiroma withdrew her arm. "I know she doesn't like you much, but it's wrong to say she hates you."

"She stole my inhaler. She knows I can't manage without it."

"Well, it wasn't really stealing. More like larking around. She didn't mean any harm."

"Well, I only said I thought it was her."

"That's not what the teacher thought. I think you should tell the teacher that you made a mistake."

Melanie was silent. She thought it served Claire right if she did get into trouble.

Shiroma said, "Look, we're all sorry for you, but you told a lie, and you can't expect us to stand by and see Claire punished for something she hasn't done."

"I never!" said Melanie. "She did it, so there!"

The nurse wasn't particularly pleased to see Melanie because she had a badly grazed knee to attend to. So Melanie sat down in her usual chair and used her inhaler, and let the cats come to sit on her lap.

The black cat was pleased. "You showed her!"

The white cat wasn't so sure. "Do you think Shiroma was right?"

"Claire deserves everything she gets."

"Even if it was her — and I'm not sure it was — then was it right to get her into trouble? That's twice this week. You've made an enemy, my girl."

Melanie muttered, "I don't care!"

The nurse said, "What's that? Are you feeling all right now, Melanie? Is someone fetching you home? I hope you go straight to the doctor this time."

Melanie was silent. What good were doctors? What good was anything? What good was going home, when her mother was in a frenzy of preparation for the wedding?

The black cat said, "You shouldn't let them push you around like this."

Melanie said to the cat, "But what can I do?"

The nurse said, "Talking to yourself, Melanie? Did you get a knock on your head when you fell?"

"I'm all right," said Melanie. But she knew she wasn't.

A man was working in the front garden, attacking the overgrown hedge with an electric cutter. He was a big man, wearing a clean but stained boiler suit.

Melanie was told to go out and ask if he wanted a cup of coffee, and when he turned round and switched off the cutter, she saw that it wasn't a strange man. It was David.

"Hi, little 'un," he said. "No, I don't want any coffee. But I could do with a hand here. Could you put all this stuff in the plastic bags I've brought? The heavy-duty ones in the boot of the car. I'll take it all back to my place. I've got one of those machines that grind up garden waste."

"You can't use privet for compost," said Melanie. "You can't use it for anything."

"Really? I didn't know that. Poisons the soil, does it? Your mother said you were a bit of a gardening buff. I'm rather new to it, but I must say I enjoy it. My old gardener retired this year, and I've been tackling most of the jobs around the place myself. I've got one of those diesel-powered mowers with a seat on it, to do the lawns, and I want to change the garden around, put in some herbacious borders and that."

Melanie felt a stir of interest. It might be fun to help him remake a garden. If only she didn't feel so tired. He didn't really want her. He was only trying to make friends with her. That was all.

He started to stuff the cut-off pieces of privet into the bags and she helped him. He didn't talk while they were doing it. She liked that about him. He wasn't always gabbing on, or having to hook himself into a personal stereo or something.

He said, "I'm a bit bothered about these roses. They haven't been pruned for years, by the look of it. Your mother said you'd been responsible for keeping the back garden tidy. It looks quite good, to my untutored eye. But these . . . so much dead wood and disease. I think some of them ought to be grubbed out, don't you?"

"Wouldn't it make the garden a bit bare?" She looked at the cut-back hedge. Pale ends of cut stems stood out from the old brown wood of the branches. There were hardly any leaves left.

"That'll soon recover," said David. "This time of year, it's still growing. You'll see, in a couple of weeks, before the frosts stop growth, there'll be new leaves all over that. And we'll be able to walk up the path without getting showered with water."

He bent down to cut away a rotten piece of wood from a rose. It snapped off in his hands and he threw it into a sack. He was wearing heavy-duty gloves to protect himself. Even the dead wood of a rose bush could give you a nasty scratch.

Melanie thought, *Why is he doing this? He'll never see the roses bloom again. We'll all be gone from here long before they show any new growth. I'll never see them bloom. All my lovely roses. All my rose petals . . . all gone.*

She went back into the house and up to her room.

6

THE SHOE BOX

Melanie leaned against the bedroom door and watched her aunt packing.

"Couldn't I come with you? I'd be ever so helpful, and go to a London school nearby and not make any trouble."

Bet shook her head, not looking at Melanie. The room looked awful with the pictures off the walls, and makeshift curtains at the window. Bet sat on her suitcase, to close it. Melanie helped her.

Bet put her arm round Melanie, and they sat there, close together, each absorbed in their own set of miseries.

Finally Bet said, "Well, this won't get us anywhere." She went to the built-in cupboard and took down a shoe-box. Bet blew the dust off the box, and gave it to Melanie.

"There. Karen tells me you've been asking after your father. I'm glad you've remembered him. Karen thinks I threw these away, but I couldn't. It's only right that you should have something of his. Don't tell your mother. She's got enough on her plate, what with the house and the new job and the wedding and everything. Did she tell you our buyer backed out? Bad luck, that. But nowadays . . . Where's my blue jumper, do you know? Ah, there it is. Take the box into your own room, will you? You can talk about it later with Karen, after the wedding, when things have calmed down. You like David, don't you?"

Melanie clutched the box, and didn't reply.

Bet gave her a hug, and kissed her cheek. "David's nice. Hang on to that. He's a poppet, take it from me. You're very lucky, and so is your mother. I told her so, but . . . Just take it easy, eh?"

Melanie got as far as the door with her precious box before Bet stopped her again.

"Listen, I've been thinking. This is a bad time for both of us, you as well as me. My job, the house, moving down South. Having to find new friends, new job, new place to live. We're in the same boat, aren't we? I feel as if I'm treading water, with nowhere firm to put my feet. But it's exciting, too. It's what I've always wanted, to get out into the world. I'll think of you. And you won't forget me, will you?"

"It would be all right, if only you'd let me come with you. I know it would."

"I know what you mean," said Bet, not looking at Melanie, "but it wouldn't be right."

Karen shouted up the stairs, "The taxi's here!"

Bet had sold her car, because she needed the cash for her fresh start in life. Most of her things had already gone off in a van to be stored until she found a place to live, and in the meantime Bet was going down to London by train.

"'Bye, love," said Bet, grabbing her coat, suitcase and holdall, and staggering down the stairs.

Melanie went through into her own room over the front door, and watched while Bet was kissed and put into the taxi. And driven away.

Then Melanie sat on the bed and took the lid off the shoe-box.

Old diaries, a scratched wooden pencil-box, a bulging folder of photographs, newspaper cuttings, letters, cuff-links, a watch, a pen.

She touched them gently. She picked up the top diary and sniffed it. Real leather, a hint of soap, a trace of oil?

She closed her eyes and tried to remember. The smell hung around her, blotting out that other one, the awful smell of burning that hung in her nostrils most of the time.

She leafed through the diary, but it was uninformative. Business appointments, mostly. The writing was large, hasty but legible. The other diaries were the same. The pencil-box had been incised with the initials R.W. The newspaper cuttings recorded Robert Wainbridge's marriage to Karen Thomas, and the birth of their daughter Melanie.

The photographs. Melanie turned the folder over. At last she was going to know what he looked like. The top photographs were of a baby on a rug. Was it her father, or herself? She couldn't tell.

"Melanie!"

The box was wrenched out of her hands. Melanie grabbed at it, and the contents spilled out all over the bedroom floor.

"Where did you get this? You naughty girl! How could you! Oh, how could you! Haven't I always said . . . You wicked, wicked girl! No, I don't mean that you're wicked. Of course I don't. Don't cry, darling. You know tears upset me. There, there. We'll get rid of these things . . . oh, they make me shudder, they really do! It's no good hanging on to the past, is it?"

Karen scooped up everything in sight, stuffed it into the box, and ran down the stairs. Melanie followed, shivering so that she had to hold on to herself. She was crying, but she couldn't get any words out to stop her mother. Melanie knew what Karen was going to do and, with the inevitability of a Greek tragedy, she did it.

She went out on to the cracked patio at the back and set light to the box, using match after match, stirring the burning paper with a stick until the little heap of relics was just a pile of ash.

Only then did Karen realize that she was crying, too. She mopped herself up, blew her nose, twitched her skirt straight and patted her hair.

Melanie saw her mother returning to the house and fled up the stairs, gasping for breath, on hands and knees at the last. She reached the sanctuary of her own room and fell on the bed.

Karen came in and moved about, picking things up and putting them away.

"Now don't cry. That's silly. It's best to put the past behind you. You'll understand, later. I suppose Bet kept that box. I thought it had been thrown away. I didn't want you to be reminded . . . I could kill Bet for giving it to you, especially now, when . . . but things will be better soon, you'll see.

"Would you like to move into Bet's room? You could, now she's gone. Not that it will be for long, of course, but you could spread your things out a bit. Well, perhaps, on second thoughts, better not, because I shall need to put the coats there next week, for the party. All my friends want to come, of course,

57

and there'll be some of David's friends, too, though God knows what they'll make of this dump. But not to worry, eh? We'll soon be out of here."

She sat on the bed and put her arm around Melanie. Melanie knew that her mother didn't feel happy about touching her. There was a difference. You could always tell. After a while Karen got up and went downstairs to make some more phone calls.

The black cat came to sit on the pillow by Melanie's head.

"Burn, burn, burn!" said the black cat, enjoying himself.

"Wake up, wake up!" said the white cat, dabbing at Melanie's cheek with his paw. "You've got to wake up."

"Burn everything down!" observed the black cat. "That's all she ever does."

Melanie gave a silent shriek and tried to get her head under the pillow.

"Come on, come on," said the white cat. "You're missing something."

"Nonsense," said the black cat. "Give up. You might as well be dead."

"Bless us and save us," said the white cat in a comical tone. "'Ark at 'im, will you? Doom and gloom. We're not dead yet and we've no intention of dying just to please you."

"Oh, shut up!" snarled the black cat.

Melanie sat up. "Shut up, both of you!"

Her movement dislodged something that fluttered to the floor. Something papery. Something blue. An airmail letter. The cats stretched out their necks to look at it.

"Burn it, burn it," muttered the black cat, twitching his whiskers with annoyance.

"Open it, open it!" sang the white cat, pressing against Melanie's arm. "Come on, slowcoach! It won't bite."

Melanie watched her hand as it inched across the bed and crept down to pick up the letter. It was one of the letters from the box. There had been a whole pile of them. This one letter must have fluttered out and hidden itself when Karen grabbed the box. If Karen knew that it had escaped her, she'd be furious. She'd take it and burn it, as she'd burned the others.

Melanie snatched up the letter and stuffed it under her pillow, listening with all her might. What was her mother up to? On the phone? Yes. There went the ping of the phone being put down. Her mother's heels rapped around the hall. Her mother's voice called up the stairs.

"Melanie, I have to go out to a meeting. See if you can scrape up something for supper, there's a dear. You'll be all right, won't you?"

"Yes," said Melanie.

"Rightio. I'll bring you back something nice, if I've time to get to the shops."

She went out, clacking her way down the front path, slamming the car door, screeching away from the kerb. She always parked too close to the kerb. A fire engine faded away into the distance, going down the main road.

Melanie sat up and took the letter out of its hiding-place. The writing was the same as that in the diaries. Her father's writing. The letter had been written to her mother at an address in Melbourne, Australia. It was dated June, two years before.

Melanie opened it up.

"Oh, my," remarked the black cat. "Reading other people's letters! Sneaky, that."

"Yes," said the white cat, sadly. "But remember that Bet wanted Melanie to have all the letters. Especially this one."

"Burn it, burn it," said the black cat, but he sounded rather half-hearted for once.

"Read it," said the white cat, climbing on to Melanie's lap, so that he could read it, too. "You can skip the lovey dovey bits, can't you? The bits where he says he's missing her so much. They're none of your business."

Melanie read the first couple of paragraphs and saw what the white cat meant. Her father was missing her mother "something chronic". He was trying to be both father and mother to Melanie, but it was hard going. Bet called in twice a week to make sure he was cooking the right sort of food, and to do their washing. He'd gone after his fourteenth job and had been short-listed, and then turned down.

"An out-of-work bum," said the black cat. "Told you so!"

"It takes guts to keep on trying," said the white cat.

Melanie read on. Her father was trying to get the new kitchen fitments in before Karen returned. A neighbour had asked him for an estimate to fit out her kitchen. Maybe he'd move into full-time carpentry and not try to get back into his old line of business.

"Told you so," said the white cat. "Not a bum at all."

Melanie stroked the white cat to keep him quiet.

He wrote that he'd taken Melanie to a family service at the local church, and they'd both enjoyed it. He wanted to take Melanie on a regular basis, and the child wanted to go because one of her best friends did.

. . . Now, my darling, I know we agreed not to indoctrinate Melanie at an early age, but she is growing up fast, and how can she make an informed judgment if she has no facts to go on?

I want her to find out for herself what the love of Jesus means. I'm ashamed of all the years I've been living without letting him guide me. I've had time to think about this while you've been away, and when you come back, I want us to talk about it. I want to commit myself to him, all over again. In the meantime, I'm going to take Melanie with me to church, and I'm going to tell her about Jesus, and buy her a book for her to read herself. I'm going to kneel down and pray with her every night, and the first thing we'll pray for is your safety, so far away.

My darling, I do miss you so. Hurry back . . .

Melanie wept.

And the white cat licked the tears from her cheeks.

7

WHERE IS MY FATHER?

So now she knew what her father was like. She read the letter over and over, until she knew it by heart. It was a wonderful letter, and he had been a wonderful man. No wonder she'd been feeling so alone without him around.

She thought about the divorced families that she knew. Quite often the father — or sometimes the mother — went away and the children never saw them again. Sometimes they had letters or post-cards, or birthday presents. That did happen. But sometimes it was just as though the father or mother had died.

Melanie shut out the word "died".

. . . it was just as though the father or mother had forgotten them.

But Melanie didn't think her father could have forgotten her. It must be all Karen's doing that he didn't come to see her any more. She thought it was just like Karen to want to wipe out all trace of her ex-husband. All that talk about "understanding it better when you're grown up".

Who did Karen think Melanie was? A first-class idiot?

For the first time in days, Melanie felt fully alive. She jumped off the bed and ran down the stairs, forgetting her inhaler, forgetting everything.

The house was empty of people, but full of their traces. Somewhere there should be her father's current address. Or perhaps (here Melanie paused) perhaps Aunt Bet knew where he was. Karen wouldn't want Melanie to know, but Aunt Bet would understand and tell her. Yes, that would be the thing to do, to write to Aunt Bet. Her address must be in one of her mother's books, perhaps scrawled on a piece of paper and stuck behind a mirror, or among the cups on the shelf in the kitchen.

Melanie searched and searched, but found nothing to help her. She realized that she might well be looking at the address, but not know that it was her father's. Or Aunt Bet's.

She could have cried with frustration.

The black cat said, "I told you so! Give it up."

Melanie gritted her teeth. She heard them grate inside her head.

The white cat curled itself around her legs. "Go on, go on. Don't give up now."

Her eyes fell on the big oak chest in the window. It was very old. Aunt Bet said it had been in their family for ages. It was a blanket chest, but they didn't keep blankets in it because they all had duvets now. They threw the odd thing in there that was too good to give away for jumble, that was all.

Melanie took the usual heap of papers, books and cigarette packets off the top of the chest, and opened the lid. Inside was the pile of letters from her mother which she'd slid in, time and time again. Melanie lifted them out and propped them up against the empty vase on the window-ledge.

Underneath was a right old mess — books, magazines, dog-eared scripts, a bunch of folders, packets of paid bills, a sweater Bet had been looking for, some leather gloves . . .

Melanie picked things up, looked at them, and put them down again. What was she looking for, anyway?

She didn't know.

"Burn it, burn it," said the black cat, crossly.

"Come on, come on," said the white cat, jumping down into the chest, and rubbing its chin against the spine of an old book.

"That one?" said Melanie, rather doubtful.

She pulled it out. An old school atlas. Useless.

The cat was now rubbing against a book which had been underneath the atlas.

Melanie pulled it out with some difficulty, took a quick look at it, and threw it back. It was a child's book, a gaudy pink and primrose-coloured book for young children. It was no help at all.

"Thank goodness that's over," remarked the black cat.

"Don't give up now," said the white cat, frantically pawing at the book.

"But it's yukky!" protested Melanie. "I hate yukky books."

She replaced the lid and the papers that had been on top of the chest and went out to the kitchen to get some milk. The kitchen looked a lot less tidy since Aunt Bet went away, and a faint haze of cigarette smoke hung over everything.

Melanie looked at the scratched kitchen surfaces, at the units which didn't match, and wondered what had happened to the kitchen her father had been working on before he left home.

It bugged her.

Eventually she went back to the sitting-room, opened the lid, rescued the children's book, and took it up to her bedroom. Inside the cover was a book-plate which said: *This Book was Awarded to Robert Wainbridge for Good Attendance.* Below was the name of the church he had attended as a small boy.

It had been her father's book when he was a child, and somehow it had got overlooked in the general clear-out after he left home.

Melanie opened it.

It was stories about Jesus.

She sighed, and threw it down. Then picked it up again. Maybe Jo would like it. Jo liked all that sort of thing.

No, she couldn't give it away. It had been his. One day, when she saw him again, she'd give it back to him. Perhaps he'd ask her if she'd read it, and she'd have to say . . . Well, no. Not quite my style. Or words to that effect.

But he'd really wanted her to read it, hadn't he? He'd actually said in his letter that he wanted her to go to church, that he'd tell her stories about Jesus and all that.

It would be like rejecting him, if she rejected his book.

She sighed and flicked through the pages, until her eye was caught by some words. She put the book down and tried to concentrate. Somewhere inside her head, way back, she could hear a man's voice tinnily scratching away, like a record with the sound turned down, reading the words on the page.

" . . . for Jesus was never too tired or too busy to have the children around him . . . "

She opened her eyes and looked at the picture. It was still a yukky book, but she supposed it must have been nice for those children to have Jesus open his arms wide, and sit them on his knee, and love them.

She read on, craning nearer the window as the light failed. The book took her into a world in which, no matter what went wrong around you, there was someone who still cared for you. It gave you rules for living and loving.

Living and loving. She could hear her father's voice saying that. She smiled, and leaned back. Living and loving. He'd said, "They're the same thing, Melanie. Living with Jesus inside you, trying to do what he wants you to do, listening to his words . . . Loving . . . "

There had been more, but she couldn't remember, no matter how hard she tried.

She looked up. It was almost completely dark in the room. She hid the book under her pillow. She was supposed to make her own bed. Her mother wouldn't look there.

Then she went down to see if she could find something for supper. Tomorrow she would tell Jo about her find, and they would talk it over. Jo knew a lot more than Melanie did. Jo had been good to her, had offered to pray for her. Melanie saw now that Jo had been doing something very big in offering to pray for her. She wished she hadn't been so rude in return. It had turned Jo off her.

Everything would be all right, tomorrow.

But it wasn't.

Melanie saw Jo and Shiroma meet at the top of her road. She ran to catch up with them, but it seemed they weren't anxious for her to walk with them.

"Guess what!" she said, breathing hard because she had had to run to catch them up. "What do you think I've found?"

Shiroma turned her shoulder on Melanie, and said something to Jo about the new games show on TV that night.

Melanie said, "What's the matter? Is something wrong? I wanted to tell you that I've found one of my father's books!"

Shiroma and Jo exchanged looks, and didn't reply.

Melanie went red, and stamped her feet. "Oh, be like that, then! I thought you were my friends!"

"We were," said Shiroma, "but we're not now. We were just talking about you, if you must know. Everyone's talking about you. There's going to be a meeting in the playground at break. We have to decide what to do."

"Why? What?" said Melanie, but she knew, really.

"About the lies you told. Claire got into awful trouble, and was she mad! She came and asked us about it, and we told her what you'd said to the teacher. Claire's got it in for you, all right!"

"So what! See if I care!"

"You see what I mean?" said Shiroma to Jo. Jo wasn't looking happy but she nodded agreement.

Melanie tried to put her own side of the case. "People shouldn't throw fireworks, especially when other people get asthma." She coughed, feeling the familiar tightness descend upon her.

"That's just it," said Jo, sounding upset. "It wasn't Claire. It was that awful boy from 3R. Claire found out who it was, but she couldn't tell the teacher, could she? And now she's got three detention periods and it's all your fault."

"I don't believe you," said Melanie, but her voice came wheezing out.

Shiroma gave her a cool look. "I said you'd go on lying about it, and I was right, wasn't I? So now we've got to decide what to do about you."

Melanie got out her inhaler and used it. Jo and Shiroma started walking away from her, but after a minute Jo stopped and looked back. Shiroma went on. Melanie walked up to Jo, hoping for a kinder word.

Melanie said, "Jo, I know it sounds bad, but I honestly didn't mean to hurt Claire."

"Maybe. I don't know," said Jo, swinging her school bag awkwardly. "But you did get her into trouble."

"But we'll still go on being friends? I need to talk to you, about the book I found, about your saying you'd pray for me . . . "

"Much good that did! Listen, I'm not having you make fun of me again!"

"I wasn't!"

"I'm sorry about the asthma, and I've tried to make allowances for you, and even to talk to you about Jesus. And this is what happens!"

"I'm sorry," mumbled Melanie.

"Sorry enough to do something about it? To admit you were wrong? To tell the teacher, and apologize to Claire?"

"No!" shouted Melanie. "I'm sorry if she got into trouble, but she did do it, and I'm not sorry I told on her!"

Jo shrugged. "Well, that's it, as far as I'm concerned.

They're talking about sending you to Coventry at school. They're going to take vote about it at break. I wasn't sure what to do about it, but now I am. I'll go along with it, if that's what they want!"

8

ALTERNATIVE
ARRANGEMENTS

Melanie didn't even turn her head as the fire engine swept by, its bell clanging. Rotten book, she thought. All lies. All that about Christians loving one another. The book had said that you could tell a Christian by the way they behaved. And look at Jo!

No one except the teachers spoke to Melanie all that day. The drama teacher called her in and said he was replacing her with someone more reliable. Life looked blacker than usual.

For a little while she'd thought there might be an answer to her problems, but it had been a false hope. The book was false. Her mother had been right. It would have been better to have burned the book. If she wanted a way out of her troubles, she'd have to find it herself.

Melanie turned the corner into their road and saw that a man was tacking a SOLD notice on the board outside her house. She didn't care. She had made a plan.

Her mother was in, on the phone as usual. There were stacks of boxes and crates in the hall. Some of them had been packed up with old clothes, discarded shoes and handbags to go to the charity shop, or the dump. Karen was beginning to clear the house.

At the same time packages wrapped in pretty paper were beginning to arrive. Early wedding presents, or late engagement presents, or both. Altogether, there were too many *things* around.

Once this evidence of the forthcoming removal would have upset Melanie. Now she went through to the kitchen and got herself a glass of milk.

David was there, watching for the kettle to boil. Only he hadn't realized that you had to press down the switch on the handle of the kettle, as well as the one on the wall. She did it for him.

He smiled at her. "Thanks. Your mother wanted a cup of proper coffee. Do you know where it is, and how to make it? I'm not much good at this sort of thing."

She helped him, feeling superior. He took the coffee into the living-room, and to Melanie's surprise, came back to talk to her.

"Look," he said, laying a jeweller's box on the table. "I've got you your bridesmaid's present. I had it engraved with your name, and the date of our wedding. 'For Services Rendered'. I hope you like it."

"Thank you," said Melanie, "but I shan't be there. It was very nice of you, of course."

David frowned. He seemed a little slow on the uptake. Melanie smiled to herself. She knew what she knew. She took her glass of milk and went upstairs to her bedroom.

But David came after her.

"Look here, little 'un," he said.

"My name is Melanie."

71

"Melanie, then. Look, your mother said she's tried to talk to you and doesn't seem to get through. She said all this has come as a shock to you, that you hadn't realized how much she and I had come to mean to one another. I blame myself. I ought to have made sure we were friends before anything was said. I want to be friends with you, Melanie. My house is lonely without children in it."

"I'm sorry about that," said Melanie, politely, "but it's not my problem."

"But when you come to live with me, in that nice room . . . "

"It was kind of you to offer," said Melanie, in her best going-to-parties voice, "but it wouldn't work."

"Look here, young 'un," said David, his voice roughening.

"My name is Melanie," said Melanie, with metal in her voice.

"Melanie, then. I don't know what you think you're playing at, but . . . "

"I'm making alternative arrangements," said this new, grown-up Melanie.

David gaped. Melanie thought he might be a "nice man", but he sure was dim at times.

"Look, little . . . Melanie. I don't know what your aunt's been saying to you, but . . . "

"David, where are you? You forgot and put sugar in my coffee! Are you up there? What on earth are you doing up there?"

David called down to her, "I'm talking to my new daughter . . . "

Melanie would have strangled him if he'd been any smaller.

She said, "Go and take a running jump, will yer?"

She'd never used such rude language before, although she'd heard it often enough in the playground. She saw him blink, and begin to get angry. He seemed to swell, almost to double in size. She took a half-step back, and stumbled over the bed.

"David, love? Come on down! I'm lonely down here without you!"

David's fists unclenched. He gave Melanie one long, considering look, reversed himself out of the door and went down the stairs. Melanie breathed from her inhaler until she was back to normal.

Then she started packing.

She couldn't take much with her, but she had a useful sort of holdall and if she was careful she could get a lot in.

But not that book. That book told lies. She would put it into one of the boxes of jumble when she went downstairs.

She looked in the mirror and smiled.

"I'm going to run away. I'm going to take all my pocket money that I've been saving for a personal stereo, and I'm going to go down to London and tell Aunt Bet that I must have my father's address. Then I'm going to live with him, happy ever after."

She made her plans carefully. Her mother was having a big, pre-wedding party, and the house would be overflowing with people, none of whom would know Melanie well. Karen had told Melanie to invite a couple of her friends from school if she liked, but Melanie didn't have any friends at school any more, so she didn't bother.

The party would occupy everyone's attention for ages, for days beforehand, and for the day after. There would be lots of people, and lots of food and drink. Melanie planned to take some of the food — not that she fancied food much — and early on the morning after the party, or perhaps during the party itself, she would slip away to the station and get on a train to London.

She went into the station and checked the times of the trains and asked how much the fare would be. She had just about enough, if she rang Aunt Bet to come to fetch her from the other end, because there wasn't going to be enough money for a taxi in London.

What she'd forgotten was that Aunt Bet would be coming back for the party and for the wedding two days later. Then she heard her mother say, "Bet can help me with that when she gets back . . . "

Better and better! thought Melanie. Now she could use all her money to go straight to her father. She'd get hold of Aunt Bet as soon as she arrived and get her father's address. Then it was heigh-ho! off to the station, and the train would take her to him, and that would be just wonderful.

Only first there was an awful row with her mother.

David hadn't told her mother about the rudeness, it seemed. But he had said Melanie wasn't happy about going to live with him, and her mother had gone through the roof. Well, wouldn't she just!

Any hint that anyone wanted anything different from what *she* wanted, and she went through the roof.

She went on and on at Melanie. "You ought to be grateful. I don't know what young girls are coming to. Who do you think you are?" Then it was, "Go to your room, I don't want to see you again till you've apologized, and David working so hard to fix you up with a holiday with some friends of his while we're away . . . "

And later, it was, "You're just trying to spoil everything. You don't even try to understand my point of

74

view! Why do you have to be like this? Why do you want to make me miserable . . . "

Melanie endured it all in silence. It wouldn't be for long. The cats sat one on either side of her holdall, waiting.

A postcard came from Aunt Bet, with a picture of a guardsman on duty outside Buckingham Palace. The card didn't have much writing on it, but just said that Aunt Bet had found a job of sorts and was going after accommodation every minute she had free, and that she'd see them on the day of the party.

Boxes of booze arrived for the party. Boxes of jumble were removed. More presents arrived. Karen's friends drifted in and out, laughing, kissing her on both cheeks, leaving presents to be opened later, leaving cigarette stubs in all the ashtrays, and dirty mugs and dirty glasses everywhere.

Karen fetched her wedding dress from the shop, and the two bridesmaids' dresses as well. She hung Melanie's dress up in her room, outside her wardrobe. Karen said "Wasn't it lovely?" and "Didn't Melanie like it?" Melanie just looked at it. She hated that dress, and everything it stood for.

The day of the party. Everyone was trying to clean the place, and making more litter as they did so.

Melanie stayed off school. She felt ill; she really did. She couldn't remember when she'd last had a good meal. Karen seemed to live on smoked salmon sandwiches and salads. Melanie didn't like smoked salmon. Or salads, much. Karen was too busy to cook properly, and didn't notice that Melanie wasn't eating.

The cats sat on Melanie's bed, watching her. There must have been a big fire somewhere near, for two engines went past in a short space of time.

Melanie got up only when she heard Aunt Bet arrive. Her mother screamed out a welcome. Her mother was beginning to lose her voice, in all this excitement.

It sounded like a mini-party going on down below — there was so much noise going on, and so much drinking.

"Melanie! Melanie, come down here at once!"

That was David, acting heavy-handed. Melanie went down slowly, leaning against the banister.

He looked angry. Everyone seemed to have stopped laughing and joking. David thrust Melanie into the living-room. There was her Aunt Bet, holding on to the mantelpiece and looking as if she wished she were somewhere else. And her mother, a gin in one hand, and a bundle of letters in the other, looking as if she were going to cry.

Yes, she *was* going to cry. What a bore.

David's hand descended on Melanie's shoulder, and pushed her towards her mother. There were some of her mother's friends hanging around, fidgeting, not looking at her. What was going on?

"My letters," said Karen, in a shaky voice. "I've just found all my letters to you. You haven't even opened them!"

Melanie didn't reply. What could she say?

"Why?" asked Karen, sobbing into her handkerchief. "What I want to know is why? What have I ever done to you that you should treat me like this?"

"There, now," said David, letting go of Melanie to put his arm around Karen.

Aunt Bet looked at Melanie, and the message came over, strong and clear. "Now we're in it."

"I'm sorry," said Melanie, though she didn't mean it.

76

"Sorry? What's 'sorry'?" said Karen, her voice rising. "I don't know what's got into you, I really don't. Here I am, doing my best for you, working all the hours God sends, and you . . . you can't even be bothered to open the letters I send you."

Aunt Bet said, quietly, "Perhaps we could all calm down . . . we have guests . . . Shall we go into the kitchen?"

"Oh," said Karen's friends, looking at their watches. "Heavens, is it that late? We had no idea . . . "

"No. Don't go!" said Karen, clinging to their hands. "I need you. Do stay. The party's only just started, and we were having so much fun. And this is not an important . . . I mean, I'll deal with it later. Have another drink, and tell me about . . . "

Aunt Bet went into the kitchen. Melanie followed her.

Bet said, "She accused me of trying to take you away from her. She said I'd enticed you with promises that you could live with me in London. I told her it wasn't true, but she didn't believe me."

Melanie said, breathing hard, "Just let me have my father's address, and I'll go to live with him."

Bet stared at her. She sat down with an abrupt movement and burst into tears.

David came into the kitchen. "Melanie, go up to your room. I'll deal with you later. Bet, Karen's asking for you."

Bet got up and went past Melanie without a word. Melanie went upstairs and put on her anorak. She was all packed and ready to go.

She stood at the window and watched fireworks trace patterns across the sky. Firework parties were starting early this year. She could smell something burning, but she didn't investigate.

She ran her fingers over the black cat's fur, and it sent out red sparks. "Burn it, burn it," said the black cat.

"Danger, danger!" said the white cat. But Melanie didn't listen.

Cars began to arrive outside the house, to reverse, to park, to spill their contents out on to the path. Someone put a noisy dance tape into the music centre downstairs. The thud, thud of it shook the house.

"Melanie, come down and join the party!"

Melanie smiled to herself, but didn't move. No party. No wedding. Her sleeve brushed the silk of the bridesmaid's dress swinging gently on its hanger from the door of the wardrobe. Melanie looked at the dress and thought how much she hated it.

"Burn it, burn it!" said the black cat.

"Leave it alone!" said the white cat.

Melanie took her scissors and cut the dress from hem to neckline. It slipped off its hanger, and she cut and slashed and tore, wrenching it into horrible, slippery rags.

"Hurry, hurry!" said the black cat, sliding to the door. "They're all so busy, they won't notice if we sneak out the back!"

"You've forgotten something!" said the white cat, pushing it along the bed towards Melanie.

Melanie picked it up, shouldered her bag, and went quietly out on to the landing. The house shook with the rock beat, thud, thud, thud. Cigarette smoke rose greyly up the stairs. People were propping up walls everywhere, even sitting on the stairs. Other people were in Bet's bedroom, shedding coats, chatting, laughing, screaming at one another's jokes.

Melanie inched her way down the stairs, trying not to touch anyone in case they noticed her. Someone flicked ash from their cigarette and it landed on Melanie's sleeve. She froze.

"Come on, come on!" said the black cat.

"You forgot your inhaler," said the white cat. But Melanie didn't go back for it. Someone might stop her and ask what she was doing.

It was the right time to go.

9

THE TRUTH

Bet was in the kitchen, laying salad out on plates.

"What . . . ?" she said.

"I'm going to stay with Jo for the night."

"Oh, perhaps that's for the best. This is likely to be an all night do, I suppose."

Melanie got safely to the back door.

"Melanie, what you said about your father. We'll have a talk tomorrow, shall we?"

"Yes, all right. Or now, if you like. What I mean is, I only need to know his address."

She couldn't think what was the matter with her, running away without having got his address. Suppose she had got to the station before she realized!

"I can't give you that. You know why, really, don't you?"

"No."

"What's that?" said one of Karen's friends, coming into the kitchen for some ice. "What's the kid on about? Isn't her father . . . "

Melanie shut out that word.

She turned and walked out into the cool night air, leaving the noise of the party behind her.

She heard someone come into the garden behind her and call her name, but Melanie had melted into the bushes at the end of the garden by then. She knew the way. No one knew the way better than she did.

Under the lilac and round the tall red rose. She could smell the fragrance of the lilac. She could smell the fragrance of the red rose. The flowers were dead, the petals she had collected long since pounded to pulp, but she could still smell them.

She inched open the gate into the alley at the bottom of the garden, and squeezed through. She could see the two cats ahead of her, their eyes gleaming as they turned their heads to make sure she was following.

"Down, down, down!" said the black cat. "Down among the dead men!"

"Fire, fire!" said the white cat. "London's burning, London's burning!"

"Look yonder, look yonder," said Melanie, smelling cordite from the firework party down the road. "Fire, fire! Fire, fire! Pour on water! Pour on water!"

The alley was overgrown. No one used it, nowadays. The backs of garden sheds loomed against the sky. Leafless shrubs crooked their arms overhead. A rocket went up close by and Melanie jumped. She was right beside one of the firework parties in the road. On the other side of the hedge, someone was barbecuing sausages. She could hear girls' voices, some of which she knew.

She crept on. It would be awful if they saw her.

The alleyway petered out in a jungle of nettles and beaten-down weeds, grasses, tin cans and abandoned rusty dustbins . . . an ancient settee, springs plopping out of mouldering covers.

A garage belonging to an empty house stood at the end of the alley. Its doors had been standing ajar, crookedly aslant, for as long as Melanie could remember. No car could get down the alley nowadays, and she couldn't remember a car ever being inside the garage.

Local children used it occasionally as a meeting-place, but it wasn't very nice, being rather smelly at the best of times. There was a window, but it was cobwebbed over and didn't open.

But tonight the garage was sanctuary.

Melanie looked around her. The party was in full swing in the garden nearby. She could still hear, faintly, the noise of the party from her own house, way back down the road.

They wouldn't miss her for ages. She was safe.

She slipped into the hut and made for the darkest corner.

She wasn't hungry, which was just as well since she had forgotten to bring any food with her. There was a big wooden crate in one corner, and she made a nest for herself in that.

There was something in her hand. A book? She couldn't remember having brought a book. Ah, that was what the white cat had wanted her to bring. Well, it was too dark to read, anyway. She curled up in a ball and invited the cats to come into her arms.

"Burn, burn!" whispered the black cat, curling up in her lap.

The white cat was agitated, running up and down. "Oh, my whiskers and woe! Don't go to sleep! Danger! I can smell it!"

Melanie could smell something burning, too, but

she was so used to it, that she couldn't be bothered to investigate. She had to think, to decide what she was going to do in the morning.

But she was too tired to think clearly.

Somebody laughed, and cut the sound off. Melanie sat up, breathing tightly. That had sounded very close, almost as if . . .

She screamed.

Something was pressed to the window above her head. A face? But no face she knew looked like that. She felt as if her lungs were being held in a giant's hand, and squeezed . . .

She cast about her, frantic to find her inhaler, but of course she'd left it behind.

The face disappeared, and Melanie realized it had been the squashed-up face of someone pressing their nose to the glass.

The doors wavered, and grated. Someone — something — outside was pressing them shut against the weeds and rubble that had been dumped in the doorway.

Melanie scrabbled back inside the case.

"That's it . . . lift and push! All together: one, two, three . . . push!"

An excited whisper. Melanie could not swear that she knew the voice, but she suspected . . .

A giggle, a lot of whispering, someone saying "No!" quite loudly. The sound of a match being struck.

"No!" screamed Melanie, realizing that another firework was going to be thrown at her.

"Serves her right!" shouted a voice she really did know. Claire.

A hizzing, fizzing something came arcing into the shed and landed on some litter.

Tags of dried orange peel, lolly sticks, paper sweet wrappers, a screwed-up newspaper.

Flash! The newspaper caught light.

Crack! The firework exploded.

Claire screamed, "How do you like that!" Something heavy banged against the door, and then . . . and then . . .

Smoke.

The black cat wailed, rushing round the area which was alight, screaming. Then he disappeared.

The flames spread. The noise of the fire was loud in Melanie's ears.

Time went backwards.

"Daddy!" She was screaming, running up the stairs. "Daddy! Save me! There's a fire!"

The white cat said, in a tender, resolute voice, "Lord, I love you more than anything in the world."

The cat's voice grew louder. He himself grew. He was as tall as a man.

He *was* a man.

He bent over Melanie and picked her up, holding her against his heart. She could feel his heart beating.

He said, "Lord Jesus, keep her safe. Jesus, I love you. Into your hands . . . "

Everything went white and silent around her.

And then, she understood.

Everything was white and silent around her. She opened her eyes and everything remained white and silent around her. Her left arm burned. The fire was inside her arm.

A woman in a cap and mask came and looked at her.

"Good girl," the woman said, and removed an oxygen mask from over Melanie's face.

Melanie went on breathing: in, out. In, out. No problem.

There was a quietness within her. She understood. Only, her arm burned.

She wasn't sure where she was at first. But it didn't matter. She knew she was safe.

When she woke up next, she knew she was in hospital. There were brightly patterned curtains and lots of flowers. There were other children, too, some as quiet as she was, and others playing games on the floor, or sitting round tables.

She tried to sit up, and couldn't. Her muscles had gone to jelly and her arm burned. They brought her some food and she tried to eat, but couldn't. They asked if she remembered what had happened, but she couldn't, not really.

They talked over her head at one another. They gave her pills and dressed her arm, and were very bright and jolly.

A policewoman came and asked Melanie if she remembered what had happened. Melanie could, sort of, but she wasn't sure, so she shook her head. She asked the policewoman how she'd come to be in hospital. The policewoman had a nice, very clean face. She said that a resident in Melanie's road had spotted a derelict garage on fire and called the fire brigade.

Some children at a nearby bonfire party had told the firemen they'd seen a girl sneak into the garage. They said they didn't know how it had got on fire . . . probably a firework going the wrong way?

The firemen got to Melanie just in time to save her life.

Did Melanie know how the garage had been set alight?

Melanie thought about it. She thought she remembered hearing Claire's voice, but she might have been mistaken. She'd made a mistake about Claire once before. She'd known she ought to have admitted her mistake, but she hadn't, and that had lost her the only friends she had in the world.

No, said Melanie, it was all fuzzy. She couldn't remember.

At visiting time her mother came with David, falsely jolly, bringing her flowers and fruit and magazines. Melanie could see the sparks of anger in their eyes, even while they tried to be nice and kind to her. She asked what day it was. It was their wedding day. Yes, they had been married that morning as planned, but they wouldn't be going off on their honeymoon, not with Melanie in hospital.

Melanie said, "Do go. I'm quite all right here. They want to do some tests and keep looking at my arm. Do go."

They argued a bit, but Melanie could tell by the way they looked at one another they'd been thinking about going anyway. It seemed Karen was more keen to go than David was. David stood over Melanie, and stroked her good arm and hand. He wasn't very good at it, but Melanie remembered that it was some time since his children had been small and in need of comfort.

She thought she might get to like him, one day. Perhaps.

So Karen and David went off on their honeymoon, after checking with the nurses that Melanie was in no danger. They said they'd cut their honeymoon short. *Maybe*, thought Melanie. *Maybe not.*

It didn't matter. She had a lot to think about, and she felt too weak to do much thinking at any one time. She got the nurse to get the book from her locker and put it on the bed by her good hand. Apparently she'd been clutching the book when she was found, and hadn't let go of it even when the fireman picked her up and took her out into the open air.

One odd thing. Her asthma seemed to have vanished. Perhaps it was the drugs they were giving her. And perhaps not.

In the afternoons a part-time nurse came on duty — an older, black woman. As she walked down the ward, she spoke to and touched every child. Their faces turned to her as she came in, and those who could, ran to hold her hand or skirt. Melanie waited for her turn.

When she got to Melanie's bed, the nurse touched the book under Melanie's arm, and said, "Hello, my pet. I see you brought your book along for comfort. I had one just like that, when I was a child."

Melanie looked into the woman's face, and understood that the love she saw there was the love of Jesus, spilling over on to everyone around her. Once you'd seen it, you couldn't mistake it.

"It's a baby's book, really," said Melanie.

"Sure, honey, it's a beginner's book. But it's all there, isn't it, all the best stories. Which is your favourite?"

"The one where he wanted the children to come to him, even when his friends said he was too tired to see them . . . "

"He probably was tired, honey. Tired almost to death. People naggin' at him all the time to do this and do that. They hardly gave him time to eat . . .

And I hear you've just been peckin' at your food. Do you think that's what he would have wanted for you? No way. He'd have said, Now eat up, and be a good girl, like Nurse Buttercup says . . . "

"You're not really called 'Buttercup', are you?" said Melanie, laughing.

"You'll see what I'm called, if you don' eat up everythin' I give you . . . " and she straightened out Melanie's sheet with a heavy, tender hand.

Melanie fell back against the pillows. She was still very frail. She said, "Oh, I'm so mixed up. I wish someone could take me apart and put me back together again."

"Why, if you need it that bad, just you ask Jesus to do that little thing for you. He's better at it than I am."

"But would he? You don't know how awful I've been, and how stupid. I want . . . I don't know what . . . "

"I know, honey. You take a look at yourself one day, and you don't like the look of what you see. It makes you kind of humble, but that ain't bad. Knowing you're not much of anything, that's a good place to start. Just you trust in him. Just you put yourself in his hands. He'll do the rest."

"That's what my father did," said Melanie, yawning. "I don't know why I can't keep awake. He died, you know."

The last thing she saw before she fell asleep, was Nurse Buttercup's loving, smiling face.

10

VISITORS

At the end of the week Melanie was sitting up, although still feeling white and shaky. The doctors said she was suffering from this and that, and urged her to eat and drink. Her arm was getting better, but was taking its time, and they thought that maybe she'd have to have a skin graft.

Cards and flowers arrived from her mother and David every day, but she didn't bother much with them. Aunt Bet sent two nice cards and came to visit her on Saturday morning.

"You're looking better," said Aunt Bet, kissing her. "You gave us all such a fright! I wanted to stay here and look after you, but your mother and David said they wouldn't be going away. And I'd only just started my new job, so . . . "

"Well, they did go. I wanted them to. It's quite all right."

Aunt Bet frowned and looked away, playing with her hair. Obviously Aunt Bet didn't approve of their going away, but couldn't say so. Adults had to hang together. Melanie quite understood that.

Aunt Bet said, brightly, "Well, the good news is that I really like my new job. It's much more interesting than I expected, and they pay good wages down in London, I'll say that for them, although of course, the price of flats . . . But when the old house is sold . . . Yes, the new buyer looks as if he can scrape together cash, which means that it may all go through quite quickly. I'm going to come back here at weekends for a bit, to make sure you're all right. David said I must stay at his house, and he's helping me to find a flat in London through his business contacts."

Melanie thought Aunt Bet was looking well, livelier than usual. She'd done her hair differently, and got some lipstick on. It made her look more like Karen than she usually did.

" . . . the place I'm staying, some friends of Karen's, they really want me to stay on, so that I can baby-sit for them occasionally, and they don't charge me much by way of rent, so I can save up for when I find a place of my own. And then perhaps you can come down to visit me in the holidays."

"I'm all right now," said Melanie. "I'm not going to cause you any more trouble. I just want to know exactly what happened to my father."

"Oh darling, must we?"

"Yes," said Melanie. "You see, I think I can remember, but I'm not clear. I remember bits, but when I try to think about them, to fix them in my mind, they slip away. You know the shoe-box full of his things that you gave me, well, Karen burned them, all but one letter. That's all I have of him."

"Yes, well." Aunt Bet crossed and re-crossed her legs. "You shouldn't call your mother 'Karen'. It's not right."

Melanie looked at her aunt, and thought that she was more of a mother than Karen had ever been.

"Well, what do you want to know? We went to the same school, your father and I. In the same class. He was always a quiet, thoughtful sort of man. You take after him, I suppose. He was a draughtsman in a big factory on the other side of town. He married Karen, and they had you, and got a nice little house near the factory. I had a flat nearby, and I used to baby-sit for you quite a lot after Karen went back to work. I used to pick you up after school sometimes, and take you swimming and to ballet classes.

"Then the factory was taken over, and your father was made redundant. Money was tight. Karen had always been clever, and she had a chance to go to Australia as continuity girl with the film unit. Your father said she must go, that he'd stay at home and look after you, and keep trying for another job. So she went. She didn't like leaving you; please try to remember that, Melanie. She loves you dearly."

"Mm," said Melanie.

"Well, there was an accident. Your father was in the garden, working on the lock of that old chest, the one we have in the living-room of the present house. He used to keep all his bits and pieces in it: old bills, papers, school books. He was always doing odd jobs around the house. He was putting in a new kitchen, I remember, when . . . Well, a neighbour saw it all. She was in the garden, chatting to him over the fence. He'd put on some chips for lunch. You were playing in the house with your kitten, such a pretty little thing . . . "

"Was it white?"

"No, I don't think so. Tabby, I think. Anyway, whether the kitten upset the pan, or you did, no one

91

knows. But suddenly they heard you screaming for help and he ran in . . . The neighbour rushed to dial 999, she could hear you screaming upstairs . . . You must have run up to get away from the flames . . . or perhaps after the kitten. Your father threw you out of the upstairs window, but . . . that was the last . . . the smoke, you know. You can be overcome by fumes so quickly, and well . . . that's it."

"And the kitten?" said Melanie, needing to know everything.

"The kitten as well. The house was gutted. Only the chest remained, sitting in the middle of the lawn at the back. When I got to you in hospital, you were very ill. You didn't know me. They said there was some concussion, and that was why you couldn't remember. Later, you knew us but didn't ask for your father, or seem to remember what had happened. The doctors said it was possibly hysterical amnesia. That means that you'd shut out what had happened, that you'd deliberately forgotten.

"Karen wanted to fly back, but of course we hadn't any money for the air-fare, and the insurance wasn't up to date, so . . . the company were very good, paid for her to come back. She came to stay with me, and we visited you every day.

"Karen was distraught. She didn't know what to do with herself. I thought she'd do herself an injury. They were such opposites, you know, but they'd always loved one another, never looked at anyone else. David was marvellous. His wife was my best friend at school, and we'd always kept in touch. Sadly, she'd died a couple of years before the accident. Cancer. She'd been ill for a long time. And their two children, ever so bright, both went off to university. So David was suddenly very much on his own. He tried to help us sort ourselves out. He found us our present house. He wanted to lend us some money to get a better place, but we couldn't let him do that.

"We moved away from the old neighbourhood, and you went to your present school when you'd recovered . . . or when we thought you'd recovered. Karen went back to work. We all thought it would be best. She didn't want to leave you. She said you were all she had left. You'd always been very quiet, but after the fire you were almost withdrawn. The doctors said that if you got worse, you'd have to have treatment, but Karen was against that. She didn't want you messed around with. If you didn't want to talk about it, then neither did she. After a while, she couldn't bear to have his name mentioned, so . . . maybe we were wrong, but we acted for the best."

Melanie tried to remember the fire, but it wouldn't come clear in her mind. Bits of it would come to the surface, but not as a connected whole. She could remember the feel of his arms about her, as he lifted her out of the smoke. And what he said before he threw her out of the window.

Melanie said, "He was a Christian and he loved Jesus."

Aunt Bet said, "Yes. He used to talk to me about it, especially towards the end. He started to take you to church. I went with you, once or twice, but after . . . I couldn't. Karen was so set against all that sort of thing. He used to tell you stories from the Bible. I don't suppose you remember. I have a children's Bible that he bought for you. Karen was going to throw it away, but I kept it. You can have it when you come to visit me."

"Will you let me have it? I want to be like him, in every way."

"He was a lovely man," said Aunt Bet. "There was talk of giving him a medal for saving your life, but Karen was against it. I would have liked you to have had a medal. It would have been something to remember him by. I mean, now that you can remember. It's two years now. You've grown up, since then. He'd hardly know you. I think you've grown even since you've been in hospital, haven't you?"

"I don't think I'll be able to get into my old clothes."

"David will buy you some more. Now you'll try to like him, won't you? And be kind to your mother. She does try, poor dear, but . . . Now she's got married again, things will be easier for her, and she'll be able to relax, not drive herself so hard. I know it won't be easy for you . . . though it's a lovely house you're going to live in, and there'll be foreign holidays, I expect . . . "

"I'd like to come to you for the holidays. I know you'll be working, but I can keep myself busy during the day, and get a meal ready for when you come back at night."

"You have to give them a chance, Melanie. And I'd be scared to leave you alone during the day, till you're older."

"And then can I come down to live with you, and find myself a job in London? Perhaps we can have a little cat."

"Why not?" said Aunt Bet.

Nurse Buttercup removed the book from under Melanie's hand. Melanie woke up with a start, and clutched it back.

"Don't! That was my father's book."

"How you getting on with it?"

"OK." Melanie felt wretched, and it showed. "It's just that . . . well . . . it's all lovely and I wish I could be like that, but I can't. The more I read, the more I realize how awful I've been."

"So?" The nurse seated herself beside Melanie, and held her free hand, stroking it, leaning her elbows on the bed, loving her.

"How can you bear to touch me?" said Melanie. "I killed my father."

"Mm. Your father had a choice, didn' he? He coulda left you to die, and stood there, cryin' his eyes out."

"He wasn't like that! He couldn't have just stood there and not done anything!"

"Well, then . . . like I said, it was his choice. What do you think he'd say, if he could see you lyin' there, cryin' and wringin' of your hands . . . ?"

Melanie spurted into unwilling laughter. "He'd say I was being stupid. He'd say to get on with it."

"So that's what you have to do, honey. If he had his time over again, I reckon your father would still have gone into the flames to save you. He knew what he was doing. Now why don't you talk to the doctors about it, honey? They're just aching to help."

"They can't help," said Melanie, pushing the bedclothes back with an impatient hand. "They don't think it's important that he was a Christian."

"An' you do, honey?"

"I want to be like him. But I'm afraid if he saw me now, he'd be ashamed of me. I'm just so . . . yukky."

"Mm-hm. You think he don' love you still, faults an' all?"

"I've been so stupid, and silly, and mean-minded."

"You done any worse than Peter?"

Melanie blinked. "You mean Simon Peter, Jesus' friend? My brain's so stupid. I can't quite remember . . . "

"When Jesus was in trouble, Peter disowned him. Said he didn't know Jesus from Adam. Said it three times. When he realized what he'd done, he was so almighty ashamed, he went away and cried. Jesus forgave him, as he forgives every one of us if we're really ashamed of ourselves, and ask him to forgive us. He goes on lovin' us throughout, but if we turn away from him, then we shut ourselves off from his love, we can't feel it, no matter which way we twist and turn. Until we turn back to him. And then everythin' comes right again."

"You don't know what I've done. I got a girl into trouble. I lied about it."

"So, you got a tongue, haven't you? You put it right. You tell Jesus you're sorry, and you tell the girl you're sorry, and then you get on with being one of his followers."

"Oh, I wish I could! Follow him, I mean. It must have been so simple to follow him, when he lived. But now . . . I wouldn't know how!"

"The Bible tells you how, honey. You read it, and you talk to him. You make time to listen to what he's tellin' you, and the instructions come through loud and clear. Why, what do you think I'm doin' right this minute, but followin' him? He said to me, 'Get off your backside, girl, and get down to that hospital, and give me a hand with all those sick children.' And here I am. Right?"

Melanie began to cry. She held on to the nurse tightly, and the nurse held on to her. When Melanie was calmer, the nurse bent over and kissed her. It was like being kissed by Jesus. *Maybe*, thought Melanie, drowsily, *Jesus had kissed her, through the love of the nurse*. It made her feel quite different, inside.

11

FRIENDS

Aunt Bet brought Melanie some notelets, and she wrote to the Headmaster of her school, to Claire, and to Jo. She explained that she had made a mistake in saying it was Claire who had thrown the firework at her, and that she wanted everyone to know.

She slept better that night than for a long time, feeling that she'd probably lost any chance of getting back into their good books, but knowing she'd put herself right with Jesus.

Knowing that made everything seem much easier to bear. Even having the dressing changed on her arm became a less agonizing affair.

The very next day, Jo came to visit her in hospital, bringing some flowers.

Jo looked shaken when she saw how thin and white Melanie was. "Help, I didn't realize . . . they didn't say you were that bad. Melanie, I want to say . . . "

"No, let me. I'm sorry, Jo. I wasn't at all nice to you, when you offered to help me . . . "

Jo went beetroot. "Listen, you've got to be joking! I'll just burst, if you don't let me say it. There was I, pretending to be such a good Christian, and you . . . "

"I didn't understand . . . "

"I should have stood by you. We all knew you weren't well . . . "

"I'm better, now."

"You don't look it."

Melanie held out her hand. "I'm OK. Honest."

Jo didn't take the hand. "But I've got to tell you . . . I heard the girls talking, at the bonfire party . . . saying they'd seen you going down the alley. I said I wouldn't help to give you a fright, because that's what they meant it to be, you know. They had no idea that the place would go up like that . . . and they were so scared when they came back! I'd gone into the house, you see. I didn't want to know about it. Then Shiroma's mother saw the flames, and she got on to the fire brigade, and everyone was so frightened!"

"But you didn't tell the police who'd done it?"

"No. I said I didn't know anything about it. I feel awful."

"Don't. I asked for it in a way."

"You didn't!"

"Don't let's talk about it any more. Tell me what's been happening at school . . . "

There was a funny sort of silence. Jo was looking at the end of the bed. There was a large bunch of flowers standing there, and behind it was . . . Claire.

Claire was also rather hot in the face. She looked at Jo, and Jo mumbled that she had to go, but would come back the next day. She grabbed her school bag and went.

Claire didn't sit down. She said, "Before you say anything . . . "

"No, let me say it," said Melanie, smiling. "You didn't mean it, and it just got out of hand. Right?"

"No, I did mean it. I meant to hurt you. And then it got out of hand."

"Same here."

Claire thought that over, and nodded. She hooked up a chair and sat down.

"So, how's the play getting on?" asked Melanie.

"Fine, except that two of the kids are off with chicken-pox, and the character they dug up to prompt is so spaced out we're all wishing you were back again."

"Really?" Melanie couldn't quite believe that.

"Yes, really."

Perhaps Claire did mean it. Perhaps she was only being polite. To Melanie's surprise, they had a good gossip, until it was time for Claire to go.

"Well, I suppose you'll be back at school soon?"

"No. They want me to have a good rest. I have lessons here, you know. They want me to be up to a certain weight before they let me go home. And then David wants to send me to another school."

"Me, too. I mean, I'm going to the private school on the common after Christmas." They looked at one another, thinking about the coincidence. Then Claire said, "I suppose they wouldn't send you there, would they?"

"I don't know. They said it would be boarding school, but I'd hate it. Would you mind very much, if I came to your school?"

"It isn't *my* school. Sure. Why not? It's not easy, starting over. Having someone to go around with, someone you know . . . that would be all right."

Melanie pulled herself straighter in bed. "Say, Claire, don't know if you're interested, but we've got a heated swimming-pool at the new house. Do you think you and Jo would like to come out and try it, some time?"

"Sounds all right," said Claire, impressed. "We'll keep in touch then. OK?"

Melanie watched Claire leave, and thought, *Perhaps we'll be real friends, one day.*

"Well, say something!" said Karen. "David went to a lot of trouble to do your room up for you. There's your own kitchenette, and music centre and TV and study area and settee and everything."

"It's lovely," said Melanie, looking around her. "Thank you, David."

She had grown a couple of inches while she was in hospital, and was wearing almost-grown-up clothes, but she didn't feel that she was filling them out yet. Any more than this beautiful, teenage dream of a room was right for her.

"It's a beautiful room," said Aunt Bet, smiling at Melanie. "I shall think of you, enjoying all this, when I'm back in London, hard at work. Did I tell you I've joined another dramatic society? They have semi-professionals in it, and give shows at the Town Hall!"

"Here's something else for you," said David, also smiling. Everyone was smiling and on their best behaviour. David produced a tiny, squirming ginger kitten from behind his back, and dropped it into Melanie's lap.

"Oh!" cried Melanie. For a moment she was so surprised that she couldn't keep smiling. This tiny scrap wasn't the least bit like her old cat, and when she'd thought of having another kitten, she'd thought of having one exactly like the old one.

"Surprise!" said David, smiling fit to split his face.

"Surprise!" cried Karen, clapping her hands.

Melanie looked from one to the other. They had meant to please her. They would be hurt and upset if she didn't show pleasure, but honestly, deep down, she didn't want this kitten. It just wasn't the right sort. But, looking up at them, and at Aunt Bet's anxious smiling face, Melanie thought that she couldn't reject their gift, or it would seem like rejecting them.

They did love her, and they were trying to show it.

She did love them, and she must try to show it, too.

She took a deep breath, and prayed, *Help me, Jesus. Make me big enough to do the right thing. Help me to love them so much that I shall love the kitten, too. Jesus, I do love you. Help me . . .*

And as she said it, Melanie realized that she did love Jesus. He was real to her, just as he had been to her father.

The kitten pounced on her little finger and began to suck it. Melanie was so surprised that she cried out, "Oh, look what he's doing! Isn't he the funniest, dearest little thing?"

"That's all right, then!" said David, giving Karen a hug. "Just for a moment there, I was afraid . . . "

"He's lovely," said Melanie. "He's just what I wanted. What shall we call him?"

"Tom Thumb?" suggested David, sitting down beside her on the new settee.

"Sinbad?" said Karen. "Bother, I forgot. I've got to make some phone calls." She drifted out.

"I must get ready," said Aunt Bet, kissing Melanie on the top of her head. "I'm catching the six o'clock train."

"I'll take you to the station," said David. Then he and Melanie were alone. They looked at one another. Melanie thought, *What I say now is going to make all the difference to how we get on. I wish I knew how he felt about me, and my dad, and Jesus.*

"One thing," said David, clearing his throat, "I've been meaning to say to you . . . What I mean is, people don't change easily. Your dear mother just has to keep herself busy. She'll be in and out a lot, maybe away from us more than we'd like. It doesn't mean she doesn't love us."

Melanie nodded.

He went on. "Your aunt, too. She's got her chance at last. I mean, I could probably have wangled her a good job up here, but she must get away, not stay here looking after you. We've got to let her go."

Melanie sighed. It was true.

"That leaves you and me," said David. "How do you feel about it, now you've got used to the idea?"

Melanie went on stroking the kitten, who had curled up and gone to sleep in her lap. She said the first thing that came into her head. "It would be hard to go away to school and leave the kitten."

David looked surprised. "Your mother I didn't think you'd want to stay at home. This boarding school is supposed to the very best. My kids went to it."

"I thought you had got a housekeeper, so that Karen could do her job without worrying about the house. I'd feel so lost away at a boarding school. If I promise not to be a nuisance, couldn't I stay here and go to the school on the common?"

"You're sure you wouldn't be bored, staying at home? You'd still be alone a lot, and housekeepers aren't the same as family, are they?"

"But you'd be around, wouldn't you? And you said you did the garden yourself. I thought, maybe, I could help . . . ?"

"Great!" said David, grinning. "We'll tackle it together!"

"There's one other thing." She got out her father's letter, and explained what it was, and how she'd come by it. David read it through, and handed it back to her.

"Your father was one of the biggest men I've ever known. That letter is just like him. I wish he'd asked me for help to get another job, but he didn't. I never even knew he'd been made redundant, until after the fire, and then it was too late."

"You wouldn't mind if I talked to you about him, now and then?"

"I'd be honoured."

"And would you let me go to church with Jo?"

David seemed to get bigger. "We'll go together. We'll ask Karen to come, too, but if she doesn't feel ready then we'll go, just you and me. I have been going, Christmas and Easter, but the rest of the time I didn't think about it. What your father said, well, he was right. You can let the most important thing in your life slide away from you, without realizing. And come to think of it, I have felt that I was missing out on something. Yes, Melanie. We'll do that. Anything else?"

Melanie shook her head. While he was reading the

letter, it had seemed quite natural for him to put his arm around her. It was still around her, and she still didn't want to move away. She thought that they'd made a pretty good start.

With a bit of help from above.

NOTHING EVER STAYS THE SAME

Peggy Burns

Why, why, did everything have to change?

For Sandie it meant a whole new life — with the mother she'd hardly seen since she was a small child. It wasn't just that they didn't get on: Sandie's mother hated music — the one thing Sandie loved most in the world, the talent she had inherited from her father. It looked like the end of all her ambitions . . .

Peggy Burns has written a number of books for children, including *Killer Dog* and *The Splitting Image of Rosie Brown*, published by Lion Publishing.

ISBN 0 7459 1249 4

THE SPLITTING IMAGE OF ROSIE BROWN

Peggy Burns

"You might have been listening, Rosie, but you really couldn't care less, could you? . . . Just lately, you've been in a world of your own half the time," said Tim.

When Rosie's father left home, her secure and comfortable world was turned upside down. But Rosie was too proud to tell her friends, especially her boyfriend, what was wrong. She felt, like Humpty Dumpty, as if she was "breaking apart", but who would help put her together again?

Peggy Burns has written a number of books for children and adults. This is her second book for teenagers. The first, *Nothing Ever Stays the Same*, was also published by Lion Publishing.

ISBN 0 7459 1741 0

QUEST

Dorothy Oxley

"They came from another world," Jon recited
confidently, *"from far beyond the furthest star we
can see. They came in vast ships and little ships
that flew through the air. It was long ago when our
ancestors were just savages. The first Starborn
were wicked . . . then the good Starborn came and
fought to set us free . . ."*

Everyone on Rakath knows about the
legendary Starborn. Few know of their
amazing legacy. Through a chance encounter
with a stranger, Jon becomes one of the few.
   Soon the crippled beggar boy is involved in
an adventure beyond his wildest imaginings.

ISBN 0 7459 1846 8

SWEET 'N' SOUR SUMMER

Janice Brown

I felt like shaking him. Here I was telling them about a man overboard, dying probably, and no one would take me seriously. Instead of action, rescue and urgency, everything was slowing down like a wonky video in a bad dream.

Joanne's fears that her Scottish island holiday will be dull are proved wrong from the very start. On the ferry she witnesses a murder, but no one will believe her story unless a body is found. Crime on the peaceful island rarely extends beyond salmon poaching, and at first Neil and Roddy, her host's twin sons, are as sceptical as the police.

But ensuing events change the boys' minds, and they soon discover that an unsolved murder is not the only local mystery.

ISBN 0 7459 1429 2

SHAPE-SHIFTER
The Naming of Pangur Bán

Fay Sampson

Deep in a dark cave in the Black Mountain, a witch was plotting mischief: "We need something small, something sly, to carry a spell . . . and then we shall see who reigns on the Black Mountain."

Shape-Shifter, the kitten, is her victim. But, before the charm is complete, he escapes. He finds himself caught in a spell that has gone wrong and a body that is not his own.

In blind panic, he brings disaster even to those who want to help him. Only a greater power can break the spell . . .

This fast-moving adventure, full of suspense and excitement, tells how a small kitten becomes the focus of the conflict between good and evil on the Black Mountain.

It is the first story in the Pangur Bán series. The other titles (in order) are: *Pangur Bán, the White Cat, Finnglas of the Horses, Finnglas and the Stones of Choosing* and *The Serpent of Senargad*.

ISBN 0 7459 1347 4

PANGUR BÁN, THE WHITE CAT

Fay Sampson

The princess Finnglas is in the deadly grip of
the evil Sea Monster, deep down in the
mysterious underwater kingdom of the Sea
Witch. And Niall has been bewitched by the
mermaids.

Pangur Bán, the white cat, is desperate. He
must rescue them — but how can he free them
from the enchantment?

Only Arthmael can do it. But who is
Arthmael? Where is he? Can Pangur find him
in time?

Shortlisted for the *Guardian* Children's Fiction
Award in 1984, this is the second book about
Finnglas and her friends.

ISBN 0 85648 580 2

THE SERPENT OF SENARGAD

Fay Sampson

Under the spell of the evil Rhymester the once peaceful kingdom of Senargad has become a place of fear, death and destruction. Battles rage, the savage Wolf-Guard roam the country and, in subterranean caverns, prisoners are held captive by the terrible Serpent of Senargad. It seems that no one can defeat the Rhymester. . .

This is the fifth story in the Pangur Bán series. The other titles (in order) are:
Shape-Shifter, Pangur Bán, the White Cat, Finnglas of the Horses, and *Finnglas and the Stones of Choosing.*

ISBN 0 7459 1520 5